"Well, the truth is, I just don't like you very much."

Lilah spoke with no hesitation at all, meeting Eben's eyes frankly. For a second, he stared back, astonished.

And then he couldn't help it. He laughed.

Lilah looked startled at his reaction, which only made him laugh harder.

When he could speak, he asked, "How well did you like your previous boss, Mervin Yoder?"

Mervin was a fussy little man in his late sixties. Decent enough, but Eben doubted he was any picnic to work for.

She considered the question warily. Then finally said, "Some days, not so much."

"Did he know you didn't like him?"

Another cautious pause. "Probably," she admitted honestly.

Eben fought a smile. "And you worked for him anyhow. It doesn't bother me if you don't like me." In fact, it made things a lot easier. "So long as you keep up your end of our bargain, I expect we'll jog along all right."

Laurel Blount lives on a small farm in Georgia with her husband, David, their four children, a milk cow, dairy goats, assorted chickens, an enormous dog, three spoiled cats and one extremely bossy goose with boundary issues. She divides her time between farm chores, homeschooling and writing, and she's happiest with a cup of steaming tea at her elbow and a good book in her hand.

Books by Laurel Blount

Love Inspired

A Family for the Farmer
A Baby for the Minister
Hometown Hope
A Rancher to Trust
Lost and Found Faith
Her Mountain Refuge
Together for the Twins
A Family to Foster
The Triplets' Summer Adventure

Hickory Springs Amish

The Amish Widower's Surprise

Visit the Author Profile page at LoveInspired.com.

THE AMISH WIDOWER'S SURPRISE

LAUREL BLOUNT

LOVE INSPIRED
INSPIRATIONAL ROMANCE

ISBN-13: 978-1-335-93695-0

The Amish Widower's Surprise

Recycling programs for this product may not exist in your area.

Love Inspired
22 Adelaide St. West, 41st Floor
Toronto, Ontario M5H 4E3, Canada
www.LoveInspired.com

Printed in Lithuania

MIX
Paper | Supporting responsible forestry
FSC® C021394

He healeth the broken in heart,
and bindeth up their wounds.
—*Psalm* 147:3

To Russell and Ellie Brock,
our beautiful grandchildren, who have
brought such joy and laughter into our lives.
May the Lord bless and guide you always!

Chapter One

Oh, she didn't want to do this. She really didn't.

Lilah Troyer hesitated on the wooden porch outside Miller's General Store and readjusted the tote bag full of sample quilt squares on her shoulder.

Although there'd been a heavy rain last night, the morning had turned out pleasant. The May sunshine was warm on her shoulders, and the small town of Hickory Springs, Tennessee, buzzed happily behind her as people went about their weekday business.

But all Lilah could think about was how badly she wanted to run back to her rented bedroom and hide.

"What are you waiting for? You'll not sell Eben Miller any quilts from out here," Susie Raber pointed out impatiently.

Lilah shot her friend an exasperated look. "I wish I hadn't let you talk me into this."

"I know." Susie gave her arm a brisk, sympathetic pat. "But without the job at the restaurant, what choice do you have?"

Lilah sighed. None, that was what.

Not if she wanted to keep renting a room in Susie's house, which she most definitely did. She loved her quiet bedroom, and this way she wasn't crowding into one of her married siblings' homes, already bursting at the seams with their growing families.

She knew her friend would let her live there for free if she could, but that was out of the question. Susie, a widow with no children, eked out a meager living working at a bakery. She relied on the extra income she received from renting her room to local single women—usually women from other Plain communities who were getting desperate in their search for a husband. Hickory Springs had a reputation for having a good number of eligible Amish bachelors.

Thanks to that—and to Susie's talent for matchmaking—none of those women stayed single for long, so she was always looking for a new tenant.

Until Lilah had come along. She'd been with Susie for over two years now, and Susie had finally given up trying to match her with local men. Now, at almost forty, Lilah was officially on the shelf in this Amish community, where most couples paired up in their early twenties. Thankfully, she and Susie got along well, so they'd been happy enough to keep their arrangement as it was.

But without her job at Yoder's Dinner Bell, she had no way to pay for her beloved, sunny little room—unless she could talk Eben into selling her quilts in his store.

Susie cleared her throat and tapped her shoe on the wooden porch.

"All right," Lilah said. "I'm going in. But once we get inside, don't you rush me, Susie. Let me ask Eben about the quilts myself, when I'm ready. If I talk to him when I'm all flustered, I'll say the wrong thing, for certain sure."

Like she had last week at Yoder's when she'd seen some *Englisch* parents laughing while their six-year-old son licked—*licked*—the serving spoons at the buffet, one after another. She'd given them a piece of her mind, and they hadn't appreciated it one bit.

Neither had the Yoders, which was why she was in this pickle in the first place.

"Ja," Susie admitted with a wry smile. "You're likely right about that. Fine, I'll keep my nose out of it. Now, chin up. This is a real *gut* idea, if I do say so myself. Eben hasn't had any quilts to sell since his wife died, and yours are every bit as well made as Rose's were. He'll snap this offer up, and you'll both be the better for it. You'll see!"

As she spoke, Susie reached past Lilah and pulled open the door. Air puffed against Lilah's cheeks, smelling a little musty. Somebody needed to do some deep cleaning.

Susie cleared her throat.

"All right," Lilah said. "I'm going." She squared her shoulders and walked into Eben Miller's domain for the first time in over a decade.

The big, high-ceiling room was cooler than the outside, and everywhere she looked, brightly colored products were angled on wooden shelves. Jams and jellies, handmade toys, books and baking mixes, all done up in fancy packages. Miller's stock was aimed more at the curious tourists who visited the Amish community than at the Plain folks themselves.

That was one reason Lilah had steered clear of the store. But the main reason had to do with Eben himself. She scanned the store warily until she spotted him. He was a tall, strong-built fellow, so he wasn't hard to find.

He stood behind the long store counter, waiting on an *Englisch* woman. She was in her sixties, old enough to be his *mamm*, but she was batting her eyelashes at him as if she were a *maidel*.

That was nothing new. Eben had always been popular

with girls, even back when they were schoolmates together. He was nice to look at, with his blond hair and broad shoulders, and he had a friendly charm that drew people in, made them feel noticed and special.

Even people who weren't really special at all, like lonesome, blunt-spoken teenaged girls.

Lilah flinched and turned away, pretending to study the jars of jams and jellies on the shelf. Thinking about the past would only make her more nervous, and that was the last thing she needed.

Quilts. That was what she needed to think about. Quilting always steadied her.

She glanced over to the alcove of the store where Rose had given quilting demonstrations to tourists whenever her frail health had permitted. To Lilah's surprise, Rose's quilting frame was still there, an unfinished quilt stretched across it, a small chair pulled close by.

Forgetting to be *naerfich*, Lilah crossed the store to examine things more closely. She stood at the narrow end of the frame, looking over the taut fabric and frowning.

It was a demonstration quilt, useful for teaching aspiring quilters about the craft. Each square showcased a different technique or pattern. Oftentimes, such quilts were chaotic and, in Lilah's opinion, unattractive. This one wasn't. Rose Miller had been a gifted quilter with a good eye for patterns and colors. She'd managed to pull the very different squares together by using complementary shades and fabrics.

The finished quilt top had been layered with batting and backing and stretched onto the frame for quilting. Lilah leaned closer. The stitches were tiny and neat, and Rose had chosen free motion quilting so that she could stitch in a way that brought out the beauty in the various blocks.

It was an excellent choice for this style of quilt. But

the pretty design was unfinished, the slim needle tucked through the fabric where Rose had set it down for the last time before her final illness. That had been three years ago now, and there was a film of gray dust on the cloth. No wonder the store smelled musty.

Lilah straightened slowly, her eyes fixed on that silver needle, twinkling in the light. It somehow seemed both very sad and very sweet that Rose hadn't put the needle away, nor tied a knot in her thread. She'd simply poked it through the cloth to hold her place, as if she'd expected to pick it up again very soon.

"Kann ich dich helfa mitt ebbes?" Can I help you with something? A male voice spoke the standard shopkeeper's greeting just behind her, making her jump.

"Oh!" She turned to find Eben studying her, his face stern. She'd not stood so close to him in years—at church she was always careful to keep her distance. He looked different. Same blue-gray eyes, same strong jaw, but a thread or two of silver shone through the gold in his hair, and new lines creased his face. Not laughing wrinkles, these. Sorrow had left its mark.

"There is nothing for sale over here," he said.

"I know," she murmured. "I was just looking. It's a very pretty quilt. Hello, Eben."

"Lilah." Wary recognition dawned. "I did not know it was you." He glanced down at the quilt, and his eyes warmed. "*Ja*, it's pretty," he agreed softly. "But it is not for sale."

She blinked. "Well, of course not. It isn't finished."

She regretted the words as soon as they were out of her mouth. Eben winced, as if she'd stuck him with a pin. By all accounts, he had been heartbroken by Rose's death, and pointing out the quilt's incomplete state was likely an unpleasant reminder of his loss.

She struggled to think of something comforting to say.

"It's mostly done, though. Someone else could complete the quilting," she suggested. "And should, probably. You can see yourself that it's getting dirty, and it can't be easily laundered until it's finished."

That was the truth, but from Eben's expression, she was only making things worse.

"The quilt will be left as it is," he said firmly. "Is there anything else I can help you with today, Lilah?"

She swallowed hard. Oh, this wasn't going well. Perhaps she should simply give up and walk away. But—she glanced at Susie, who was inspecting the pretty bags of baking mix displayed on a wooden table—that would mean she'd also have to give up her room. And she'd come this far.

"I make quilts." She blurted out the words before she lost the last of her nerve. "*Gut* ones, too, like this one." She fumbled in her bag to bring out the sample squares she'd brought to show him. "See?" She laid them out on the demonstration quilt one by one.

The bell over the door jangled as a group of *Englisch* women came in. Eben glanced in their direction.

"I'm sorry. I can't talk anymore. I've customers."

"I sew fast," Lilah said desperately. "Fast and well. They'd bring good money, my quilts."

"I'm sure they would, but—"

"You should sell them here. I've half a dozen completed now, so plenty to stock in. And I could make more."

"Oh, are you going to be selling quilts again?" One of the *Englisch* women had drawn close, her eyes bright with interest. She called over her shoulder. "Shelly, they're carrying quilts here again! Finally! Remember that beautiful one your sister bought here all those years ago? Is this the same quilter who made that one?" The last question was directed to Eben.

"No. She is not. And I do not sell quilts in my store." Eben's deep voice cut in firmly. "Not anymore." He picked up the sample squares one by one and held them out to Lilah. "Please put these back in your bag."

"But," Lilah protested, "if you'd just look—"

"Never mind. She's not the same quilter," the woman called across the store. "Such a pity. Is that other lady, the one who made your quilts before, is she still making quilts anywhere? We're willing to drive any distance if you'll tell us where she is."

Lilah glanced up just in time to see the pain in Eben's eyes, and her heart constricted.

Eben Miller was a member of her church and her community, and as such, he merited her respect, her kindness and her help, should he need it. But she had no personal fondness for him, not since that day all those many years ago when he'd announced in front of all her friends that he wasn't sweet on Lilah Troyer, never had been and never would be. She could still feel the white-hot humiliation of that moment, made all the sharper because of the secret daydreams she'd been spinning about the two of them.

Nee, Eben Miller was not her favorite person. But the sorrow on his face just now...well. She couldn't help but feel sorry for him.

"Well?" the woman prompted impatiently. "Is she still making quilts someplace?"

His throat pulsed. "No, she is not."

A hefty sigh. "Are you *sure*?"

"For pity's sake," Lilah said. "That woman you're talking about was his wife, and she's *dead*. So, *ja*. He's sure."

"Oh!" The woman's eyes widened. "Oh, I'm terribly

sorry. I...had no idea. Shelly? Girls? Let's go. I...uh...for-got something in the car."

In a few seconds, the whole group was gone, leaving Susie the only other person in the store. She stared at Lilah, hor-ror on her face, a checkered bag of muffin mix clutched in her hands.

Eben's lips tightened. He held the stack of quilt squares out to her again.

"Take these and go home," he said evenly. "I don't sell quilts here anymore."

Then he turned on his heel and walked away.

Eben pretended to be busy behind the counter, but he watched Lilah out of the corner of his eye as she stuffed the quilt squares back into her bag. She stopped briefly next to Susie Raber for a whispered conversation, and even at this distance, he could see that Lilah's cheeks were bright pink.

He'd upset her. Eben sighed as he straightened the items next to the cash register. He hadn't meant to. It had just... stung him a bit, the way she'd spoken so matter-of-factly about Rose.

She's dead.

Of course, she was. And it had taken some time, but Eben had made his peace with that—mostly. But now and then something would happen, something simple like a woman commenting innocently on Rose's last unfinished quilt, and the old grief would rise up and wash over him in a wave. He did his best to keep his pain to himself when that happened, but sometimes in spite of his best efforts, it splashed over onto other folks.

Lilah finished talking to Susie and hurried out the door, but Susie didn't follow. She placed the bag of apple cinnamon muffin mix back on the shelf and walked up to the counter, her usually friendly face set in stern lines.

"That," she said as soon as she was close enough, "was not very nice, Eben Miller."

He sighed. "I'm sorry. But it's true what I told her. I don't sell quilts."

"Maybe not, but you could have been nicer telling her so." Susie tilted her head, looking at him with eyes that reminded him sharply of his late *mamm*. "She's having a hard time just now. She lost her job at Yoder's Dinner Bell, and she's in need of money."

"Oh." Now he felt worse. "I didn't know."

"Maybe you didn't know the particulars, but you should have figured something was wrong. Otherwise, would she have come here asking you for help? It's not as if you two are *gut* friends."

Well, no, they weren't. Not since the day he'd found out that Lilah had been telling the other girls that he was sweet on her.

He hadn't been, although he'd liked Lilah well enough. Her habit of saying things out loud that most folks only thought in their heads had bothered other people, but it had amused him.

So he'd been kind to her, not meaning anything special by it. By then he'd fallen head over heels for delicate little Rose Lapp. But one night when he'd asked to drive Rose home after a singing, she'd echoed the rumors he'd already been teased about by the other boys.

I thought you'd be seeing Lilah home, Rose had said, her face creased with disappointment. *So I told Sam I'd ride with him.*

Sam Zook, his biggest rival for Rose's affections, had smirked as he walked out to hitch up his buggy.

So, *ja*. Eben had said it loud and clear. *I'll not be driving Lilah Troyer anyplace, Rose, not tonight nor ever.*

He'd meant it. But as he'd stalked out to claim his own buggy, he'd caught a glimpse of Lilah's face.

She'd looked...stricken. And afterward—even all these years later—she ducked for cover whenever she saw him coming. He'd always felt bad about that, but he'd never had an opportunity to make amends.

Until today.

"I'm sorry," he repeated.

"I'm not the one you should be apologizing to." Susie drew in a long breath. "You've had your share of pain, Eben, losing your Rose so young. And I'm sorry for it. But maybe next time you remember that you're not the only person in the world with troubles, *ja*?" She bustled out the door just as another group of *Englischers* came in.

Eben was busy the rest of the afternoon. His store was beginning to be noticed by the tourists who'd recently discovered Hickory Springs' small Plain community, and he did a brisk business most days. But all day, whenever he had a spare moment, his mind drifted back to Lilah, and his conscience pricked him.

"I've been waiting in line for ten minutes," an older *Englisch* lady said grumpily just before closing time. "You need to hire some help, young man."

Eben forced a smile. "I'm sorry. I usually do have somebody else working, but my last helper...uh...quit a few days ago."

Trudy Schwartz had quit, all right, when it finally sank in that Eben wasn't in the market for a new wife. Except for the inconvenience of running the store alone, he wasn't overly sorry to see her go. Trudy was a nice enough woman, but it was clear what she wanted, and since he wasn't interested, things had grown a bit awkward between them.

She was the last in a long line of women, widows and never-marrieds, who'd applied to work in his store over the past couple of years, many of them urged on by *mamms* or *aents*, convinced that Eben would be ready to remarry at any moment.

As if wives could be replaced as easily as shoelaces.

He normally closed the store around six, but it was half past before he finally locked the door. He'd have to hire another store clerk and soon, or things would come unraveled quickly.

As he walked down the street to the little stable where he rented a stall for his horse Blaze during the day, his mind drifted between his two troubles: the unpleasantness with Lilah and the pressing need to hire a new store clerk.

Preferably one already safely married.

That last part would be difficult. Married women were usually busy at home with their *kinder*. Rose had only been able to work with him—when her fragile health permitted—because *Gott* had never seen fit to bless them with a family.

As Eben hitched Blaze up to his buggy, an idea occurred to him. He turned it over in his mind as he went through the mindless routine of buckling the straps. It was an uncomfortable idea—and unexpected.

But the more he thought about it, the more sensible it seemed.

So when he and Blaze clopped out onto the street, instead of turning toward home, they headed in the opposite direction.

Toward Susie Raber's house.

Chapter Two

"Asking Eben Miller for a favor." Lilah thumped her over-flowing basket of quilt pieces onto Susie's well-scrubbed kitchen table. "I should have known better."

Her cheeks had stung with embarrassment the whole drive back. Not only had Eben refused to even look at her quilting, but she'd also managed to say just the wrong thing, as usual.

She couldn't decide which one bothered her more.

"*Ach*, well." Susie was retying her black bonnet under her chin. "Our plan didn't work out so *gut*, maybe, but it was no favor you were asking. Eben used to make a tidy sum selling Rose's quilts in the store, and so naturally I thought he'd be happy to have another source for them."

"Apparently not." Lilah muttered. She began setting the pieces out on the long wooden table.

Susie watched her for a second. "Are you sure you don't want to come to my *kossin*'s supper? Erma will be happy to have you."

"*Nee*, but thank you. I'm planning to spend a quiet evening piecing some squares together. I'm agitated after talking to Eben, and quilting settles my nerves."

Susie sighed. "Please don't stew over it, Lilah. I gave Eben an earful after you left, but we mustn't be too hard on him. He and Rose were a very devoted couple. Such a grief runs deep, and like a weed, it can pop back up when you least expect it."

Susie spoke matter-of-factly. Susie's husband had died only three years after their marriage, long before she and Lilah had become close friends. Susie rarely spoke of her late husband, John, so the loss must still pain her.

"Still," Susie went on, picking up the wrapped strawberry pie she was taking to Erma's. "While we'll always remember the folks we've loved, hard grieving is only meant for a season. It's past time for Eben to move on with his life, maybe find himself a new wife."

A new wife? A horrible thought occurred to Lilah, and she froze, her fingers crumpling a deep red triangle. "You didn't send me to Eben's store because you were trying to match the two of us up, did you?"

That idea hadn't occurred to Lilah but it should have. Shortly after she'd moved in, Susie had tried to match her new renter up with three different fellows—and the results were disastrous. She hadn't tried again, and Lilah had assumed her friend had given up on the idea altogether.

But from the half-defiant, half-guilty expression on Susie's face, maybe she hadn't.

"Susie!"

"Would it have been so bad?" Susie asked irritably. "Eben's a *gut* man who makes a nice living, and you're a kind, hardworking woman. There's no reason you both should be lonely."

"Eben Miller and me? A couple?" Lilah didn't know whether to laugh or throw her pincushion at Susie's nose. "That's just…silly."

"I'd have thought you'd be pleased," Susie muttered as she headed for the door.

Lilah frowned, stung. Was Susie casting her past mistakes up to her? "Why would I be pleased about such a thing?" she asked sharply.

"A man like that is like catnip to most *maidels*. Why do you think so many have hired on to clerk in his store? They were hoping to catch his eye, that's why." Her friend shook her head and sighed. "But our Eben's a hard nut to crack."

Lilah relaxed—a little. "Well, I'm no cat and no young *maidel*, either. I've no interest in catnip or Eben Miller. And he certain sure has no interest in me."

"Pity," Susie said over her shoulder as she left the kitchen. "On both counts. But suit yourself."

Left alone in the kitchen, Lilah tried to focus on the quilt she was piecing. It was to be a star design, which meant a lot of precise cutting and careful sewing. She needed to pay attention if she wanted this quilt to be pretty enough to sell.

Although, she wasn't sure where she'd sell it or the half dozen others she'd stowed in a trunk in her bedroom. Hickory Springs was only just beginning to be noticed by tourists fascinated by the Plain lifestyle, and Eben's was the only store in town that catered to them. There were other, better established Amish communities with similar stores, but surely they already had quilt suppliers. She could try advertising, maybe, but quilts, to Lilah's way of thinking, sold themselves better when the buyer could see and touch them.

She sighed. It was a problem. Of course, she could go and live with one of her siblings. Four of the six lived close by, and any of them would make room for her if she asked. But her brother Jacob already had their *daed* living with him, and her sister Ella had her husband's parents. Her other two siblings had rapidly growing families, and space in their homes was hard to come by. If she lived with them, she'd have to share a room with her nieces, or, if she was given her own room, the poor children would be crowded together even more tightly.

She didn't like either of those choices. But what else could she do? Susie didn't charge much rent for her extra bedroom, but she needed every penny. Without a job, Lilah couldn't—

The sound of wheels crunching over gravel interrupted her thoughts. Frowning, she glanced at the clock ticking on the wall. Susie had only just left. Had she forgotten something? Lilah tiptoed to peek out the kitchen window, and her heart skipped into a higher gear.

Eben Miller was climbing out of his buggy.

For a second, all she could do was stare and wonder. What in the world was he doing here?

An astonished hope rose in her heart.

Maybe he'd reconsidered and was willing to sell her quilts after all. Eben didn't seem the sort who changed his mind easily, but she could think of no other reason he'd be walking across Susie's yard right now.

She took a deep breath to steady herself and sent up a silent, desperate prayer.

Please, Gott, let this be good news. And, she added hastily, *help me to keep my foot out of my mouth.* Then she went to open the door.

Susie Raber's home was a nice one, Eben thought. Not too large, but large enough. Well-kept, too, in spite of the fact that her husband had been gone many years. The men of the community would have helped with that, of course, as they would have done for any widow. She'd not have to pay for repairs they could handle.

Probably a good thing. Susie couldn't be making much money at Smucker's Bakery, even though her cakes and pies had a reputation that extended well past Hickory Springs. Of course, Susie also had the rental income from Lilah.

At the thought of Lilah, Eben's stomach clenched. His idea had seemed a *schmaert* one back at the store. But now?

Now he wasn't so sure.

It was too late to back out, though. Lilah herself was opening the back door.

It felt funny seeing her standing there looking at him, like stepping back in time to his school days. He'd not paid much attention to Lilah since they were *youngies* together. She looked mostly the same even now, just a few character lines on her face, like all of them had these days.

He remembered her as an awkward schoolgirl, but she'd grown into her height, as his *mamm* would say, and carried herself well now. She was slim but sturdy-built, with an oval face and light brown hair combed neatly under her *kapp*. She had a nice straight nose and a level way of looking at a man that was somehow reassuring and unsettling at the same time.

If any woman in Hickory Springs would tell a fellow the unvarnished truth about himself—or pretty much anything else—it was Lilah.

"Eben?" Her voice lilted up with the question, but her mouth stayed straight. "I wasn't expecting to see you again this afternoon."

"I was on my way home from the store, and I thought of something I wanted to talk to you about. Do you have a minute?"

Most people would have said yes right off, but Lilah took the time to think his question over. "*Ja*, I do." She pushed the screen door wider. "Come in."

The kitchen he walked into wasn't big, but it smelled good enough to wake up his stomach. Some tasty dishes had been cooked here recently. His *mamm*'s kitchen had smelled much the same way—still did. His own at home, not so much. Rose had always been sickly, and although she'd tried her best, cooking hearty meals had been a struggle for her. Relatives had helped some, and he had too, best as he could.

His gaze dropped to the table, and his heart felt as if a fist had squeezed it. Triangles of colored fabric were scattered over the wooden surface, like fallen flower petals. Lilah was piecing a quilt. He'd walked into his own kitchen at home many a time to see pretty fabric squares laid out like that—and supper not yet started.

He'd never minded. Quilting had made Rose happy, and that was all that had mattered to him.

"Eben? Would you like a glass of lemonade?"

Lilah's polite question jerked him back to the present. "*Denki*, but no. I can see I'm keeping you from your own work, so I'd best get to my business." He turned his straw hat around in his hands as he spoke. "I was thinking about what you said in my store this afternoon."

Her slim neck pulsed once as she swallowed, and a faint tinge of pink edged into her cheeks. "I'm sorry if I spoke wrong. I didn't mean to bring up a painful memory."

"*Sell is awreit.*" He meant that—it was all right. He was used to it. People stepped on his feelings all the time. Almost all his memories were painful now, although some jabbed harder than others. "That's not what I came to talk about."

A hopeful light sparked into her eyes. "Have you reconsidered letting me sell my quilts in your store? Would you like to look at the ones I have ready? They're upstairs."

"*Nee.*" He spoke quickly because she was already on her

way out of the room. She paused in the doorway, looking back at him. "I've not changed my mind on that."

He'd not sell quilts in his store anymore. There was little enough he could do to mark his wife's short time on the earth, but the quilts at the store—those had always been hers. Their absence, for him at least, made a point worth making. Rose Miller, a sweet young woman had once lived and loved and made pretty things. Now she was gone, leaving an aching, empty space behind her.

For him at least. Other folks—even her parents—seemed to have moved on. Somehow that made him even more determined to leave Rose's little quilting corner empty.

One tiny part of the world that still belonged to her.

"Oh." Lilah's face fell. "Then why are you here?"

"I have a proposal for you."

"A proposal?" Lilah's eyes widened, then narrowed suspiciously. "Did Susie speak to you after I left?"

"She did. And she gave me an earful."

The gentle pink in Lilah's cheeks went fiery red. "Well, whatever Susie said, she doesn't speak for me. That was her own silliness. I'm not interested in any proposal you two have cooked up, so you're wasting your time."

He stared at her, thoroughly confused. "I didn't talk to Susie about this at all. This is my own idea, and I've spoken to nobody about it yet. How can you know you're not interested if you haven't heard me out? But—" he shrugged "—if you feel that way about it, I'll wish you a good evening and take myself on home."

He was halfway to the door when she spoke.

"What was it? That you were going to ask me?"

He turned. "I thought you weren't interested."

Her cheeks were still mottled red. "I'm…not sure now. Maybe I was…mistaken. What were you going to ask?"

"If you'd be willing to work in my store."

"Work in your store?" Her eyebrows went up.

"*Ja*. I need a store clerk. Customers are kept waiting too long otherwise, and I'm taking a lot of paperwork home to do as well because I can't tend to it at the store. I've other things to see to at home, and there aren't enough hours in my days lately." He hesitated, not sure how to word this next bit. "Susie said something about you losing your job at Yoder's, so I thought maybe you'd be available."

"You want me to work for you? At your store?"

She sure seemed to be having a hard time understanding him. "That's right. It doesn't pay much, but I imagine it's about the same as you made at Yoder's." He quoted a modest hourly wage. "I'll need you six days a week, but you can pick a day to be a half day, whichever you like. I'd rather it wasn't Saturday because that's usually one of the busiest ones, but any other day will work. And you can pick the morning or the afternoon off, whichever you'd like."

She was still staring at him, her brow furrowed. He sighed and added, "Or if you need a whole day off, we can work that out, too."

She shook her head, then walked to the table and pulled out a chair. "Maybe," she said, "we'd best sit down and talk this over." She quickly gathered the quilt pieces and tucked them in a basket.

He wasn't sure what there was to talk about. He'd told her everything already. But after a second's hesitation, he took the chair opposite her. "So? Do you want the job or not?"

She folded her hands on the table. "I need the job. But I'm not sure it's a *gut* idea."

The truth was he wasn't so sure of that himself, but since he was the one asking, he couldn't admit that now. "Why not?"

She looked down at her long, slender fingers, twined together on the wooden tabletop. "Did Susie tell you why I lost my job at Yoder's?"

"*Nee*. Only that you did."

She swallowed and then looked up at him, meeting his eyes as if it wasn't such an easy thing to do. "They let me go because they said I was rude to customers."

He considered this. "Were you?" It was certainly possible, but knowing Lilah, it had likely been an accident.

"Maybe, although I only meant to be firm. I fussed at parents who were letting their child run wild at the buffet. He was licking the serving spoons and—"

"*Ach.*" Eben shook his head and snorted. "*Englisch* parents, then?"

"That's mostly who comes to Yoder's. And they certain sure don't like to be told when their children misbehave."

"Sounds to me like you were in the right of it."

She darted an uncertain look at him. "It wasn't the first time I'd spoken sharp-like to a customer. A couple of times, the folks put bad reviews online because of it. The Yoders weren't pleased."

No, he supposed they wouldn't be. He sighed. He had work waiting for him at home, and he needed to finish this up. "Why are you telling me all this, Lilah?"

"Because that's why I'm not sure this is a *gut* idea. I'll likely run off half your customers in a month."

He shrugged. "Customers like that, maybe they need running off."

"And, of course, there's the other thing," Lilah went on as if he hadn't spoken.

"What other thing?"

"Well, the truth is, I just don't like you very much."

She spoke with no hesitation at all, meeting his eyes frankly. For a second, he stared back, astonished.

And then he couldn't help it. He laughed.

Lilah looked startled at his reaction, which only made him laugh harder.

When he could speak, he asked, "How well did you like Mervin Yoder?"

Mervin was a fussy, short and stout man in his late sixties. Decent enough, but Eben doubted he was any picnic to work for.

She considered the question warily. "Some days, not so much."

"Did he know you didn't like him?"

Another cautious pause. "Probably," she admitted honestly. Eben fought a smile.

Probably, nothing. Almost certainly Mervin had known. Lilah was honest to a fault and not so good at schooling her expressions.

"And you worked for him anyhow. It doesn't bother me if you don't like me." In fact, it made things a lot easier. "So long as you keep up your end of the bargain, I expect we'll jog along all right." She still looked uncertain, so he added, "If you're worried, we can do a trial day."

"A trial day?"

"You work for me for one whole day. And at the end of it, we decide if we want to continue or not. How does that sound?"

"And you'll pay me? For the day that I work?"

The anxious look in her eyes troubled him. He nodded. *"Ofkors."*

A very brief hesitation. Then, *"Ja,* I'll do it."

"Kumm to the store tomorrow at seven. I'll show you the ropes before we open up."

"I'll be there." She stood, and he did as well, clapping his hat back on his head.

"I'll see you then. *Mach's gut*."

"*Mach's gut*, Eben."

He replayed the conversation in his mind as he rode home behind his trotting bay gelding. It had gone well enough, he decided. At least she was willing to give the job a try. And by the worried look on her face when she'd asked about getting paid, the money would be a blessing to her.

That was all *gut*.

And that bit about not liking him...his lips curved at the reminder. Maybe Lilah's honesty shouldn't have made him laugh, but it certain sure had. He hadn't laughed so hard since...

His smile faded. He spent the rest of the drive home trying to remember the last time he'd laughed like that.

He couldn't recall exactly. All he knew was it had been a very, very long time.

Chapter Three

Lilah moved jars of blackberry jelly off the polished wooden sideboard and began wiping the dusty shelves. Eben had set her to cleaning as soon as she'd arrived, and she'd been working her way around the store all morning.

"It needs it," he'd said. "And I've not had much time to clean lately. While you're at it, you can watch me wait on the customers. You'll learn more that way than by me just telling you things, and the cleaning will help you see what all I stock and where everything is."

She'd agreed, but privately she hadn't thought it a very good plan. The store looked clean enough already, and customers poured in the minute he unlocked the front door, soon forming long lines that wound around the big room. Wiser, she'd thought, for Eben to have put her at the counter. She already knew how to ring up purchases—and she also knew *Englisch* customers didn't like to be kept waiting.

But after an hour or so, she decided Eben had made a wise decision. The store only looked clean. Whenever she moved items, she discovered dust, and sometimes even trash stuffed here and there by thoughtless customers.

And she really was learning a lot watching him. Some things about the store, for sure, but also a great deal about Eben himself.

They'd lived in the same community for decades, but she didn't know as much about him as she did her other neighbors. Seeing him had always reminded her of that embarrassing moment when he'd told the world that he wasn't interested in her.

She'd never been much liked by the boys, and Eben's casual kindness had meant a great deal to her. She'd spun all sorts of sweet daydreams about him, secretly, while doing her chores at home. Which might have been fine—if she'd actually kept them secret.

But, as usual, her mouth had gotten her in trouble. She'd made the mistake of sharing some of those dreams with her closest friends, and they'd talked out of turn, as teenage girls tended to do. When someone teased Eben about it, he'd wasted no time making his feelings clear—loudly, and to pretty much everyone she knew.

Although he probably hadn't meant to, he'd hurt her feelings, badly. So it was true, what she'd told him back at Susie's. She didn't like Eben much. Oh, she'd forgiven him, a long time ago. It was a sin to bear a grudge. But being around him made her feel *naerfich* and ashamed, so she'd gone out of her way to avoid him.

Until now. So she had a lot of catching up to do.

Eben, she soon noticed, was a patient man. He never acted the least bit rushed, not even when an elderly customer talked too much, with a long line of folks waiting behind her. He was fair in his dealings, too. He pointed out a little chip in a mug one lady was buying, offering to either get her another or to give her a discount. The woman hadn't noticed the damage, and Lilah could tell she appreciated the storekeeper's honesty.

But as Lilah had worked her way around the store, watching Eben out of the corner of her eye, she'd noticed something else. He smiled and kept his talk cheerful, but after a customer had turned away, his face always fell back into sorrowful lines.

Lilah wiped off a jar of strawberry jam and set it back in its well-dusted spot. Eben, she reflected, was much like his store. He looked all right on the surface, but underneath, he wasn't all right at all. His cheerfulness didn't go very deep.

Except when it came to children. With the *kinder*, Eben was different. His eyes lit up, and he always reached for the glass jar he kept beside the register, full of brightly colored striped sticks of sugar candy. He let each child choose one for free, and the smiles he gave the little ones didn't dim near so quick after they'd scampered off.

Lilah sighed. He'd have made a good *vadder*, Eben. It seemed a shame that he and Rose hadn't had any children, but such matters were in *Gott*'s hands and not something for her to question. And, of course, he could have a family yet, if he chose to remarry. As Susie had pointed out, plenty of young women would be overjoyed to have a husband like Eben Miller.

Around twelve o'clock, he followed a customer to the door, flipped the sign to Closed and locked the door. He waited on the few remaining people, unlocking the door for them to leave. When the last person was gone, he turned to Lilah. By then she'd finished with the jams and was dusting the small collection of Amish recipe books he kept in stock.

"I close for an hour at midday," he said. "To eat. I forgot to mention it."

"*Ja*, I knew," she said. "It's on your sign. I brought a lunch."

"*Gut.*" He nodded, looking uncomfortable. "There's a table and chairs in the storeroom. You can eat there, if it suits you."

She nodded. She'd seen it when she'd stowed her belongings away. "All right."

She visited the restroom to wash her hands and then went into the storeroom to retrieve the small cooler containing her lunch. She sat at the round wooden table, spread out a napkin and unpacked her simple meal.

And waited nervously for Eben to join her.

It would feel a bit odd to eat together, back here, the two of them alone. But of course, there was nothing wrong with it. They worked together, at least for today.

She uncapped her water bottle and took a sip as she considered the high-ceiling storage area, festooned with cobwebs. It needed a good, deep cleaning. Likely he'd set her to work in here once the front was done.

Where was he? At least ten minutes had gone by, and he'd not appeared. She waited another few seconds, then decided to investigate.

She walked out into the store. At first, she didn't see him. Then a faint rustle made her look to her left. Eben was sitting on the wooden stool in the quilting corner, his own lunch box on the floor beside him.

Not much of a lunch, she couldn't help but notice. A sandwich made of bread heels and a bruised-up apple. But that wasn't her concern at the moment.

She'd felt uneasy at the thought of eating with him back in the storeroom, but having him shun her company altogether? That felt worse. Still, maybe she'd misunderstood.

She cleared her throat. "I thought you said we ate lunch in the storeroom."

"I said *you* could, if it suited you," he answered without looking up. "I eat out here. Alone."

"Oh!" Well, that was certainly clear enough. Embarrassed, she retreated into the gloomy back room and returned to her spot at the small table.

The room was stuffy and had an unpleasantly musty smell. She didn't blame Eben for not choosing to eat back here, although, of course, his choice likely had more to do with being closer to the memories of his wife than anything else.

And probably a desire to avoid Lilah's company. Not that she could fault him for that. Hadn't she been avoiding his for years?

Still, it prickled a bit.

She gathered up her lunch, stuffing it back into the cooler for easy carrying. She'd had enough gloom for one day. He'd said she could eat in here if it suited her.

Well, it didn't.

She left the table and walked out the back door into the sunlight.

Miller's General Store was located on the main street, but since Hickory Springs was a one stoplight place, downtown didn't extend far beyond the strip of brick-fronted store buildings. A square patch of green grass stretched behind Eben's store, framed neatly by a wooden fence.

Once upon a time, somebody—maybe Rose herself—had planted some perennial flowers. Daisies, black-eyed Susans and a variety of other flowers grew in a pretty tangle, and a weathered bench sat against the brick wall of the building. Butterflies of different colors, blue, yellow and black, fluttered from blossom to blossom.

Lilah smiled. Oh, she loved butterflies. *Ja*, this would be a much better place to eat her lunch.

She carefully brushed off the seat of the splintery bench and sat, unfolding her napkin across her lap. Then she settled in to enjoy her food.

Not long after she'd finished eating, the door creaked open. Eben looked out, his expression uncertain.

"I was wondering where you were," he said.

"That storeroom's no fit place to eat, not until I give it a good scrubbing. It was nicer out here, with the flowers and all. I enjoyed watching the butterflies." As she spoke, she stowed her crumpled napkin and sandwich baggie into the cooler and flipped the lid closed. Then she stood, brushing a few stray crumbs off her skirt. "Is it time to open the store again?"

"*Ja*, almost." Eben seemed oddly hesitant. "When you weren't in the storeroom, I thought you'd left."

"Left? Why would I do that?"

"I was a little rude, maybe. Earlier. Eating in the quilting corner by myself." He looked embarrassed, and Lilah shrugged.

"You were." She gave her apron one last shake and leaned over to pick up the cooler. "But I overlooked it. You're like an old dog with a broken leg. Every now and then you're likely to growl, but that hurts nobody. Now, how about we go on back inside so I can get to work? The sooner I finish cleaning the front of the store, the sooner I can scrub out that stinky storeroom."

With that, she walked past him and back into the gloom of the old building.

He was a grumpy old dog who growled at people.

Lilah's description kept popping back into Eben's mind at odd moments during the afternoon. Was that really how she saw him?

He didn't think he was like that. He didn't growl at people. In fact, he went well out of his way to be nice.

But he could see why Lilah might think differently. He'd

had more short words with her in the past twenty-four hours than he'd had with anyone else for years. There was something about her that made him feel...

Well, it was hard to put a word to. Funny. Unsettled.

He wasn't used to that. His life had been settled for a good while now, once he'd gotten past the first awful year without Rose. He couldn't say he was happy, but now he was resigned to *Gott*'s will. And as he'd worked his way through his sorrow, he'd discovered an unexpected side effect of grief.

Not much disturbed him anymore.

He supposed that was because when you'd lost the person who'd mattered most, you didn't care much what else happened. But Lilah, now...

For some reason, Lilah stirred him up, the way that the cloth she was wielding energetically over the books in the bookcase stirred up the dust. He had no idea why, but all day he'd felt as swirly as the motes floating around in the light from the windows.

That was something new, something he wasn't sure what to do with.

He watched her out of the corner of his eye as the day wore on. She never slowed down, bustling around the store with every bit as much energy as she'd shown in the morning. He couldn't help comparing her to Rose, who'd wilted like her namesake by early afternoon, even early in their marriage when her health had been better.

Lilah kept going. She didn't need much instruction from him, either. Once he set her to a task, she simply completed it, figuring out things on her own. She'd asked him almost no questions the whole day.

He wasn't sure if that was because she wanted to leave him free to wait on his customers or because she wasn't too interested in any instructions he'd give. Knowing Lilah, it could have been either.

About fifteen minutes before closing, the bell over the door tinkled. He glanced up to see an *Englisch* family coming in, two parents and a scruffy-looking boy and girl.

The parents had an unpleasant look, and their expressions were set in hard lines. The boy looked to be eleven or twelve, the girl maybe half that age. Although the adults were well filled out, the two young ones were scrawny, their faces milk pale and hollow-cheeked. They looked as if they needed some square meals and a few hours in the sunshine.

"How much?" the woman asked Lilah abruptly, holding up a bag of muffin mix.

Eben started to answer himself, then decided against it. This would be a good opportunity to see how Lilah handled an unpleasant customer.

"Eight dollars," Lilah responded pleasantly. "The price is on the little tag."

"That's a rip off." The woman weighed the bag in her hand. "There's only enough in here to make one batch of muffins."

"It makes two dozen, but *ja*, you're right. It's a lot of money for muffins you have to bake yourself." Lilah continued wiping down the display of candles and lanterns, and Eben smothered a chuckle.

Small wonder she hadn't lasted at Yoder's, telling customers things like that.

"So?" The woman said. "How about lowering the price, then?"

Lilah kept on dusting. "Oh, I can't do that."

"Why not? You just admitted the price is too high."

"This isn't my store. I just work here, so I don't have any control over the prices. And I didn't say the price was too high. I said it was a lot of money for muffins you have to bake at home, and it is. But you're not just paying for that, are you? You're paying for the pretty cloth bag and the cute tag there with the recipe printed on it. That's meant to be a gift, not something you'd bake in your own kitchen. Now," Lilah went on, "if you're looking to save money on your baking, you should check out the bulk supplies over at Yoder's Dinner Bell. They're three doors down, and they keep a little store next to the restaurant. There's wheat berries and bulk spices and other things, all at lower prices than you'll find in *Englisch* stores for the same amount. Better quality too."

"Oh." The *Englisch* woman still looked annoyed, but she didn't appear to know quite what to say.

Neither did Eben. He'd forgotten to be sneaky and was staring openly at Lilah. She didn't seem to be aware of him at all, though. She was very carefully wiping down the glass globes of the kerosene lamps on display and didn't appear to think she'd said anything out of the ordinary.

"Wayne?" the *Englisch* woman said to her husband. "I want to go to that Dinner Bell place and see what they've got. This place is too expensive. Corey, Bethany? Come on. We're leaving."

The children had been examining the toy section, talking softly to each other. They looked up, and their wide-eyed expressions made Eben wince. They looked both alarmed and unhappy.

"The Dinner Bell doesn't carry things for children," he said impulsively. "Only grocery staples. And like she said, it's just three doors down. You can leave them here if you like, let them look at the toys. I will keep an eye on them, and you can collect them when you are done buying your baking supplies."

Lilah looked up then, astonishment on her face. He was a little surprised himself. He didn't know what had pushed him to make such an offer.

Had he been a parent, he'd have refused such a thing immediately. He'd never leave any *kinder* of his with someone he didn't know. But the two adults just looked at each other and shrugged.

"It'll be easier without dragging them along," the woman said.

"You can stay here if you want to, but don't set foot out of this store," the man ordered the children. "You hear me?" Both of the young ones nodded instantly, and Eben couldn't help noticing the relief on their faces.

After their parents had left, Eben nodded to the children. "Look at the toys all you like," he said. "Nobody will bother you."

They shot him uncertain glances and didn't offer any thanks. Instead, they sidled around to the other side of the toy display where they weren't so visible. Eben sighed and turned his attention to waiting on his next customer.

It bothered him to see little ones unhappy and ill fed. Not too clean, either. But he noticed how protective the boy was of his little sister, how close he stayed to her, patiently watching as she looked at a collection of little wooden animals, one by one.

That observation both warmed his heart and worried him. That boy—Corey, the woman had called him—was a loving *bruder*, but he acted more like a parent.

Which probably meant the ones who were supposed to fill that role weren't doing their jobs too well.

"I shouldn't have done that."

He turned to see Lilah at his elbow, twisting her dust rag. *"Vass?"*

"I just told those folks to go someplace else to buy things." Lilah's cheeks were hot pink. "I probably cost you some business. I'm sorry. I didn't think… I'm sorry," she repeated.

Eben didn't know what to say. On the one hand, she was right. It wasn't exactly *gut* business to send customers away—or for that matter, to agree with them that a price was too high.

On the other hand, she was right in what she'd said, and he hadn't been particularly sorry to see those two *Englischers* leave his store anyway.

"Don't fret yourself," he said finally. "We'll talk everything over at the end of the day."

Lilah still looked unhappy, but she nodded. "All right. Those two there," she lowered her voice. "Poor little things. They might need two sticks of your candy apiece, *ja*?"

So she'd noticed that, too. "I think maybe so."

They watched the children in silence for the next half hour. The little girl became fascinated by a painted wooden cat, her thin face alight with happy interest. She chattered softly to her brother, who nodded now and then, his face tight.

Those were nice toys, well carved and prettily painted by a local Amish couple. Eben's only complaint was the price, but he couldn't fault the Fishers for charging what they did. A toy like that would last for three generations, at least.

Eben kept his own profit margin as low as he could, but the price was still high. He didn't see that sour-faced woman buying such a thing for her daughter, and he suspected the boy knew that as well.

Just then, the parents came back in the door. "Come on," the woman ordered. "We're ready to go."

"Look, Momma Karen," the little girl said. "Isn't this pretty?" She held the small cat aloft, her face hopeful.

"Put it back, Bethany," the woman said impatiently. "Foster care don't pay us enough to buy you kids toys, that's for sure. And hurry *up*."

Bethany's bottom lip wobbled, but she obediently put the little cat back on the shelf and started toward the door. Her brother waited a second before following, and as Eben watched, his grubby hand flashed out to the side and back.

And just like that, the cat was gone, and there was a suspicious bulge in the boy's jacket pocket. It was so quick that if Eben hadn't been watching closely, he'd never have caught it.

"Excuse me," Lilah said, her voice strong and firm.

The *Englisch* woman had the door open. She looked back, frowning. "What?"

"Lilah." He spoke quietly, firmly. *"Du naett."* Don't.

She looked at him, puzzled. "But," she said in *Deutsch*, "what about their candy?"

She hadn't seen, then. He relaxed and nodded. *"Ja*, I was forgetting."

"What is it? We're in a hurry," the woman said impatiently.

"The children may have some candy, if that's all right. It's free," she added quickly.

The woman shrugged. "If it's free, I guess they can have it."

The children walked to the counter, and Eben proffered the glass jar. "Choose two each."

"Don't take all day," their foster mom called irritably.

The little girl picked first, two of the same kind, pink-and-green-striped sticks. Eben noticed that her brother chose a licorice one and then a pink-and-green one.

No doubt that second one would be going to his sister—along with that stolen cat.

"Come again," he said pleasantly. Tightly clutching their sticks of candy, the children walked to the door and were gone.

"Not even a thank you." Lilah shook her head.

"They don't know any better."

"No, I suppose not. And they've got poor examples to follow, from the look of things. Those were their foster parents, I'm guessing. I've heard of that. One of my *kossins* and his wife fostered some children. Very sad situations."

"Very sad," Eben agreed. He didn't like to imagine the sort of home the poor children must have come from, if living with those two was an improvement. He'd be keeping them in his prayers, for sure.

"I need to get something from the storeroom," Lilah said. "I'll be right back."

Eben glanced at the clock on the wall. "Almost time to close up anyhow. A few minutes early, but since there are no customers just now, I'll lock up and sweep off the porch real quick. We'll set the store to rights, and then we'll talk things over and see where we stand."

Lilah bit her lip. "All right."

He flipped the sign to Closed and collected the broom he kept tucked behind the counter, but before going to sweep the porch, he checked the areas she'd been working on. She'd done well. She'd almost made it all the way around the store, and she'd cleaned thoroughly.

In the children's area, he rearranged the wooden toys to cover the gap from the missing cat. He'd accept the loss and think no more of it. It was very bad to steal, of course, but that poor boy...

A tiny noise caught his attention. He stepped around the shelf to see Lilah standing behind the counter.

"*Vass* are you doing there?"

She jumped guiltily. "Oh! I'm sorry. I thought you were still outside."

He didn't answer. His eyes were fixed on the cash register. She must have opened it—something she'd no business doing.

And there was money in her hand.

Chapter Four

"What are you doing?"

Lilah's face flamed red, but she stood her ground. "I'm not stealing from you, if that's what you think," she said. "This money came out of my own bag. I'm putting it in the drawer, not taking it out."

That made little sense. "Why would you do such a thing?"

"I owe it to you. Let's leave it at that."

Eben frowned. He didn't like having to pluck this information out bit by bit, but he wasn't letting this go without an explanation.

"Why do you believe you owe me money? Did you break something?" He didn't think so. He'd not noticed any such thing, and he'd kept a sharp eye on her throughout the day. "If you did, the sensible thing to do would have been to tell me."

Maybe she'd been afraid to, fearing he'd be angry. But he'd not have held one mishap against her. Accidents happened, and he broke things himself from time to time.

"*Nee*, I didn't break anything." She lifted her chin. "But I did do something wrong. I saw someone steal something, and I did nothing about it, even though I should have."

Understanding dawned, clearing Eben's confusion. So that was what this was about.

"That boy," Lilah went on before he could speak. "The *Englisch* one who came in with his sister. He put one of your carved wooden animals in his pocket. I should've said something, but…" She trailed off, her expression a funny mix of apology and defiance. "But I didn't want to."

He wasn't sure quite what he should say, but one thing seemed clear enough.

"It sounds as if he owes me the money then, not you."

"I saw him do it," she repeated stubbornly. "And that's part of my job, ain't so? Keeping an eye out for such things. It doesn't do you much good if I see folks stealing but do nothing about it. I should have said something before he left the store, but I didn't, so it's only fair I should pay you for the little cat." She put the money in the cash drawer as she spoke, carefully slipping each bill into its proper slot.

"If you feel so strongly about it, why didn't you say something at the time?"

She kept her eyes on the money she was sorting. "I felt sorry for him. He didn't look well cared for, and he didn't want the plaything for himself anyhow. His little sister wanted it, and those parents would never have… I just felt sorry for him," she repeated. "But that doesn't change the fact that I allowed him to steal from you. Although," she muttered, "I do wish he'd stolen something else. Those wooden toys are cute enough, but I don't see why anybody buys them for the ridiculous prices you've set."

Only Lilah. Eben had to work hard to keep his lips in a straight line. Only Lilah would say such a thing as that right now.

"You can keep your money," he said as soon as he trusted himself to speak without laughing.

"Nee." She closed the cash register with a firm shove. "I did wrong, and I'll pay for it."

"You did no wrong. Or if you did, I did the same. I saw that boy take the cat myself."

She stared at him. "You saw?"

He felt slightly insulted by her surprise. "I see most things that happen in my store."

"But why didn't you say something?"

"For the same reason you didn't. I felt sorry for the child. As you said, the boy seems to be in a sad situation and most likely has never been taught to have a good character. It's wrong to steal, of course, but it seemed more wrong to make a fuss over such a small thing, given the circumstances."

She cocked her head, considering him curiously. "You're a strange storekeeper. You'll not make much of a profit if you've no quarrel with people walking off with your stock."

"I don't make a habit of it. Get your money back out." When she didn't budge, he shrugged. "If you don't, I'll just add the amount to your paycheck."

She lifted an eyebrow. "You're a very stubborn person, Eben Miller."

"I could say the same about you." He paused. "And while we're on the subject, I guess we should get something clear. If you take this job, you'll need to understand that I'm the one in charge." He wouldn't have spelled that out to most folks, figuring they understood such a thing without being told. Lilah was a special case, though, and it was always best to start off as you meant to go on. "I'll be making the decisions and telling you what to do while you're in my store. If you're going to have trouble with that, best not agree to work here."

She studied him, her hands clasped in front of her apron. "Are you offering me the job, then?"

"I am." He hadn't been sure of that until just now. She'd worked steadily today and done her job well. Maybe she spoke her mind a bit too freely, but that fault didn't bother him as much as some others.

He waited while she worried her bottom lip, an uncertain crease in her forehead.

"So? Do you want some time to think it over?" he offered finally.

"Nee," she said. "I don't need any time to think. But you might. I really need a job, Eben."

"I know." For a plainspoken woman, Lilah sure did like to talk in riddles. "And I'm offering you one."

"I need a *gut*, steady job," she went on as if he hadn't spoken. "A lasting job. I have to be able to pay my rent at Susie's because she depends on it. Like her, I've no *mann* to support me. No children. I can't afford to be choosy right now, but you can, and you already know I'm likely not the best person for a job like this. Are you sure—certain sure— that you want me to work here?"

She spoke evenly, as calmly as if they were discussing the weather instead of her livelihood. But there was something in her eyes, something in the tense way she held herself that told him she was *naerfich* waiting for his answer.

She was right, of course. In some ways, she wasn't the right person for the job. She was blunt-spoken, never a good thing when you were dealing with customers. And no matter how carefully he explained that he was the boss of the store, he felt certain she'd speak just as plainly to him whenever they disagreed on something.

Which, likely, they would. And often.

But then he recalled her trying to slip money she certainly couldn't spare into the register because she felt guilty about letting a child steal from him. Because she hadn't wanted her act of mercy to cost him anything.

So he nodded, firmly. *"Ja,* I'm sure. The job's yours if

you want it, and I see no reason why you won't keep it so long as you work as well as you've done today."

She held his gaze a minute longer, searching his face. Whatever she saw must have reassured her because she smiled. "All right, then. I accept. I suppose we've only got to decide my schedule. What half day would you rather I take off?"

"Take whatever day pleases you."

She considered. "I'll take Tuesday mornings off. That's a slow day for most businesses, so it'll be less trouble for you if I'm gone. Now I'm going to go poke around that dirty storeroom a bit, so I'll know just how to go about cleaning it tomorrow afternoon. I'll have this front part finished by then."

He frowned. "I'd planned on you waiting on customers tomorrow."

"Oh, no." She shook her head. "Best to wait another day on that. The storeroom's in awful shape, and right now you're still used to managing the front of the store by yourself. Later you'll not find it so easy to do without me."

She spoke with matter-of-fact confidence, and before he could protest, she'd whisked off to the storeroom leaving him dizzy-headed.

This woman was unlike any other he'd ever dealt with. His point about being the boss of this store sure hadn't stuck with her very long.

Knowing Lilah, he'd probably have to remind her of that pretty regularly.

He should be annoyed, but oddly enough he wasn't. Instead he felt his lips twitching again.

Working with Lilah would have its difficult spots, certain sure, but all in all he didn't think he'd made a bad bargain. She was honest to a fault, and that was no small thing.

Kind to children, too, which he valued highly. One or two of the women he'd hired had been sharp with little ones, and that didn't sit well with him.

Best of all, as she'd said at Susie's house, she didn't think much of him, so he didn't have to worry that she was angling for a wedding.

As he went to put the broom in its spot, the twitch in his lips bloomed into a smile. Lilah might not like him so much, but that was all right—convenient, even.

On the other hand, so far he liked her a good deal better than he'd expected to.

A week later, Lilah was doing her best to hold on to her patience while Eben tossed down her latest suggestion.

"I close for an hour at lunch," he repeated doggedly as he flipped the sign over.

"I know you always have. But maybe now that you have a helper, the store should stay open. We could eat our lunch in shifts."

He was shaking his head before she'd even finished speaking. "There's no need for that."

"But what about people who might like to shop during their own lunch breaks?" She'd been keeping mental track of his customers over the past week, and while he stayed relatively busy, she wasn't sure he was turning enough profit to comfortably pay his salary and hers as well. That worried her a bit because, as she'd told him, she really needed this job.

"That's why we close from one to two. Most people are back at work by then."

"But—"

"Lilah, it's decided." He spoke with a quiet firmness that

she'd learned to recognize. "And I'm done talking about it. Go eat your lunch."

She blew out an irritated sigh. "Well, I wasn't done talking," she muttered as she headed for the storeroom.

"You never are."

Eben's remark, laced with weary amusement, drifted after her. She stopped for an indignant second, then straightened her shoulders and stalked silently on to the back room.

That, she thought, was very unfair. Since starting work here, she'd been biting her tongue far more often than speaking her mind.

She wouldn't say anything else, she decided as she went to collect her lunch cooler. She was only trying to help. If he hadn't enough sense to see that, fine. Let him close the store and lose some sales if that was what he preferred. It was his business, after all, and as he'd pointed out when they'd made this agreement—and more than once, since— he was the boss.

She'd repeated that particular conversation to Susie, and to her surprise, Susie had taken Eben's side.

"He's right," she'd said briskly as she'd shaped loaves of sourdough bread into pans to rise overnight. "He has the responsibility of running the place, so of course, he'll make all the decisions. If you want to make a suggestion, I'm sure he'd be glad to hear it." At that point, Susie had looked up and fixed Lilah with a stern gaze. "Assuming you make it gentle-like and are willing to take no for an answer."

Judging by Susie's tone, she didn't think Lilah was so *gut* at those particular things. So Lilah had set out to prove her wrong. For the past week, she'd kept most of her suggestions to herself, only speaking out when it seemed really important. And she'd done her best to be gentle and polite—and to take no for an answer when Eben didn't agree with her.

That hadn't been as easy as she'd expected. Only a few of her ideas had been listened to, things like how best to organize and clean up the storeroom, for example, and that maybe a new doormat would cut down on some of the dirt tracked into the store.

But on the more important things, Eben hadn't been willing to budge. He really was a very stubborn man, Lilah thought irritably. And he was right about one thing. She had her own stubborn streak, and just then, she'd come dangerously close to giving him a piece of her mind.

She couldn't afford to do that.

She shouldn't have brought that idea up this morning, anyway. She'd been thinking about it for the past couple of days, but it could have kept awhile longer. She'd had a trying day, and she was feeling irritated and out of sorts. Her scooter had broken halfway to town, and she'd had to drag it the rest of the way. After work she'd have to find some way to get it to her brother's house. Amos was a good tinkerer, and likely he could fix it for her.

But getting it all the way over to his house would make for a long and tiring afternoon.

As she pulled her cooler down from a freshly scrubbed shelf, she was momentarily startled by the weight of it. Then she remembered why it was so heavy, and she paused, caught in indecision.

Should she or shouldn't she?

She didn't know. This had seemed a good idea in Susie's kitchen first thing this morning—a kind and sensible idea. But now?

Now she wasn't so sure.

Then again, hadn't *Mamm* always said that loving your

neighbor was about what you did, not how you felt? Maybe she was irritated with Eben at the moment, but that didn't change the fact that he brought the saddest lunches she'd ever seen a man try to eat.

She flipped open the top of the cooler, rummaged a minute and then headed for the front of the store with both hands full.

She found Eben in his usual spot, beside the unfinished quilt in his wife's old nook. Today he was peeling open the lid of a can of store-bought sausages and balancing a half-eaten sleeve of saltines on his knee. She wrinkled her nose.

He didn't glance in her direction, keeping his gaze focused on the little can. "I hope you've not come out here to argue with me more about opening the store. I've said my piece on that."

"*Nee*, I've not come to argue." She spoke quietly and in a tone so gentle that even Susie would have approved.

Seeing him sitting out here had brought their argument about closing the store into a new light. She'd not thought of that—how he always sat here during lunchtime to have his food in his late wife's favorite spot.

Likely that was why he didn't want to keep the store open. He could have no privacy here with customers roaming about.

"What is it then?" He finally got the top off and laid it carefully beside his boot on the floor. It would be disposed of, she knew, as soon as lunch was over. Eben might not be so good at deep cleaning, but he was considerate. "And can't it wait until I'm done eating?"

"Not so well, no. I've brought you something else to eat." She walked over and placed her offering on the small table beside him. "It's not much, only a couple sandwiches and some cookies. We've plenty of bread and sweets at the house, what with Susie working at the bakery and always trying out new recipes. With just two women living at home, it's hard to keep things from going to waste. I thought maybe you'd be willing to help us out."

Before he could protest, she turned and walked briskly back to the storeroom. Her duty done and her conscience now clear, she carried the cooler out the back door to the wobbly old bench where she usually ate her lunch.

She'd cleaned the storeroom thoroughly—and what a job that had been—but she still didn't think it was such a nice place to eat lunch. She much preferred sitting out here in the sunshine, watching the butterflies flitting around the flowers. Likely she'd have to move inside once the weather cooled off—assuming she still had a job by then—and so she figured she'd make the most of the fine summer weather while it lasted.

She'd only eaten half her own sandwich when the door behind her creaked open. She turned her head to find Eben looking at her, the lunch she'd brought him in his hands.

He looked uncomfortable, and she felt a prickle of exasperation.

"You know, it's plain silliness to refuse *gut* food when it's offered you."

"I'm not refusing it." He paused. "It wonders me, though, why you brought it."

She slanted him a puzzled glance. "Most people I know would have better sense than to look a gift horse in the mouth." Better manners, too, but she'd leave that part off. "I brought it because, like I said, we've too much at home, and those lunches you pack for yourself aren't half enough for a man of your size. You work far too hard to scrimp on your eating." She tucked a bit of lettuce back into her half-eaten sandwich as she spoke. "Folks may think storekeepers don't work so hard—I thought that myself. I see now that I was wrong. It's not all standing behind a counter. You unload stock off trucks and climb up and down ladders half the day. You must be starving before closing time, and I certain sure don't need you making yourself sick. Like I told you, I need this job."

"I see." She thought she saw a hint of relief on his face. "Well, then, I thank you."

"Oh." She shrugged. "*Du bisht welkom.* I hope you enjoy the food."

She expected him to duck back inside, but instead he hesitated for a second, then pushed through the door and into the sunshine. Still looking awkward, he dropped down on a wooden chair set kitty-corner from the bench. He bowed his head for a silent grace, then opened his eyes and started unwrapping one of the sandwiches she'd given him.

Eben was going to eat out here? With her? That was a startling change. She wasn't sure what to say or do, so for safety's sake, she took a big bite of her own sandwich. If she was busy chewing, she couldn't say anything that would get her into trouble.

Maybe he figured the same because he ate without talking. Still, she couldn't help sneaking little glances in his direction, and she was satisfied to see that he was obviously enjoying the food. It was nothing special, just thin-sliced ham and cheese with some lettuce and Susie's homemade spicy mustard, but compared to what he'd been eating, no doubt it made a welcome change.

"That your scooter there?"

They'd been silent for so long that she was startled when he spoke. "*Ja*, it is."

"There looks to be something wrong with the back wheel."

She laughed, earning a startled look. "I know that. It broke on the way over. I'm taking it to my brother's house after work to see if he can fix it for me."

An idea occurred to her. She thought it over as she brushed crumbs from her skirt.

She'd ask, she decided. One good turn deserved another, and it wasn't like it would be much trouble for him.

She shot Eben a measuring glance. He was just finishing the last cookie she'd brought him. *Gut.* Growing up with brothers had taught her that the best time to ask a fellow for a favor was when he had a mouthful of something yummy.

"You could drop it off for me, maybe," she said. "It's on your way, ain't so? Amos's house? It'd save me a good bit of time and extra walking."

It wouldn't be half so much trouble for him, she knew. He drove his buggy to work, leaving it at a small stable down the street.

He looked startled, but he seemed to think the request over as he chewed and swallowed. "*Ja*, it's on my way home. But how'll you get back to Susie's then?"

She shrugged. "Oh, I'll walk it. That's no trouble. The scooter just makes the trip a bit quicker, that's all." She got to her feet. "We've a few more minutes before it's time to open back up. I'm going to go put out some more jams. A good many have been bought, and that shelf's looking a little empty. Maybe you'd better order in some more."

He nodded, still eyeing the scooter. "Maybe," he murmured absently.

Lilah sighed as she walked inside the dim storeroom. She picked up a box and began collecting the jams stored in the back. There weren't too many left, since they were a very popular item. She'd try to think of some way to goose Eben into following through on ordering more. Going by that absent-minded "maybe," it wasn't high up on his list of things to do.

Of course, given how prickly he was about her suggestions, she'd have to do that carefully. She set out the jams one by one, dusting them briskly—not that they really needed it. She'd done a *gut* job in that storeroom. She arranged the jars so that they made an attractive display and stepped back to admire the effect.

Someone rattled the doorknob, and she looked over to see customers waiting impatiently. She glanced up at the clock and her eyes widened. Five minutes past time to open.

Well, that was strange. Eben was many things, but he was never, ever late.

She unlocked the door, murmuring a welcome to a handful of *Englisch* ladies. As they fanned out to browse the store, Lilah hurried back to pick up the cardboard box, planning to stow it in the storeroom.

When she reached the door to the back room, Eben was on his way out.

"You're late," she couldn't resist pointing out. "I had to unlock the door."

He lifted an eyebrow, but he didn't answer, ducking behind the counter as one of the ladies approached, a cookbook in her hand.

Lilah started to set the box down just inside the storeroom, then changed her mind. She might as well walk this on out to the trash container outside the back door. The last thing she needed was for this room to get cluttered again.

As soon as she pushed open the door, she noticed that her scooter had been moved to a different spot.

And that wasn't the only thing that had changed.

She touched the handlebar and rolled it forward. Both wheels turned without a hitch. There'd be no need for Eben to take this to her brother's house after all. He'd already fixed it for her himself.

Now, that was a real nice thing to do. Much nicer than sharing some leftovers, so it put her in his debt.

But she wouldn't stay there for long. She was going to find some way to help Eben make a bigger profit off this store of his.

Whether he liked it or not.

Chapter Five

"You don't have to do that!" Eben hurried across the store to take the heavy box of baking mixes out of Lilah's arms.

Business had slowed down, and Lilah was taking the opportunity to restock some shelves. That part he appreciated. Lilah never needed to be told what to do. She could look around the store and figure out what should be done every bit as well as he could do himself.

None of the workers he'd hired before her had been slackers, but Lilah outworked all of them. That, it turned out, caused a problem of its own. She didn't ask his permission before jumping into difficult jobs, and he was constantly having to watch her to make sure that she didn't hurt herself.

Now Lilah surrendered the box grudgingly. "I was managing," she protested, but her cheeks were as rosy as the plum-colored dress she was wearing.

"This is too heavy for you to carry," he said shortly. "I've told you before. When you need something like this brought out from the storeroom, ask me. I'll get it for you. I don't want you to put yourself in the hospital."

Lilah made an impatient face. "I've a strong back, and I know what I can carry and what I can't. You've nothing to worry yourself over."

He didn't answer because, actually, he doubted that was true. Lately it seemed that he spent a lot of his time talking Lilah off ladders, taking away heavy boxes and reminding her when it was time to go home.

He started to set the box down, then thought better of it. Lilah was right about one point—she usually was, when it came to such things—the mixes desperately needed re-stocking. Lots of bending for her if he left the box on the floor.

"Wait a minute." He put the box down and went to re-trieve a stool from behind the counter. He wasn't surprised that, by the time he got back with it, Lilah had already opened the carton and was pulling out the fabric bags of baking mixes.

"I asked you to wait," he pointed out irritably. He set the wide-seated stool down and balanced the box on top of it. "Now," he said. "Not so much bending."

He expected a thank-you—Lilah was always very grate-ful. She'd thanked him three times for fixing her scooter the other day. But instead, she simply studied the box.

"What?" he asked.

"I could've managed," she said. "Carrying the box and unpacking it from the floor."

"Maybe. But you'll tire yourself out faster, and there's no need when I'm handy to help out."

"You have plenty of other things to do." She reached back into the box and gathered an armful of the brightly colored bags. "More important things than babysitting me."

"None of which I'll get to do if my only helper is out of work with a strained back."

He thought that was very reasonable, but Lilah shot him an exasperated look.

"Oh, for pity's sake! I'm not likely to hurt myself picking

things up or bending over. I'm not like Ro—" She stopped herself, shooting him a horrified glance.

He stood frozen in his spot, not knowing what to say. For a second, they stared at each other. Then he cleared his throat.

"Nee," he agreed coldly. "You are not like Rose." Then he went to look over some bills he'd laid on the counter.

Or pretended to.

In reality, his mind was too jumbled up to focus on the numbers in front of him. Because—as was all too often the case—Lilah was right.

She wasn't like Rose, but for some reason he was certain sure treating her as if she were. He'd not even noticed himself slipping into his old habits. It hadn't happened with the other employees, but then again, while they were all good enough workers, none of them had been as energetic as Lilah.

Not even close.

He'd never worried about them hurting themselves or tiring themselves out too much, but with Rose, *ja*, that had always been on his mind. She'd wanted to come to the store with him as often as she could, and he'd allowed it because it made her happy. But he'd worried over her. Especially since, like Lilah, she'd tended to overdo.

That was one of the few things the two women had in common.

Of course, Rose had done that because she'd loved him and desperately wanted to please him. She'd felt guilty that her poor health kept her from being a strong partner in their marriage, and had blamed herself for the fact that they'd never had children who could have eased some of the load from his shoulders.

He'd never blamed her for it. But he'd never been able to convince her otherwise.

So, *ja*, he knew why Rose had tried so hard. He wasn't sure why Lilah did.

The door creaked open, and he glanced up to see a group of *Englischers* coming in. He shuffled the still unchecked bills into a pile and set them safely to the side, preparing to wait on his customers.

That group was the beginning of a pleasantly busy afternoon. He stayed behind the counter, and Lilah worked at restocking the shelves as items were purchased. They avoided each other's glances, although he caught her looking in his direction more than once.

For his part, he was glad that they didn't have time to talk. He shouldn't have spoken so sharp-like to her over a slip of the tongue. He'd have to apologize and smooth things over, best he could.

As it turned out—as was usual with Lilah—she didn't give him the opportunity to speak first. As soon as he'd flipped the sign to Closed and locked the door, she marched over, a determined expression on her face.

"I'm very sorry," she said. "I didn't mean to—"

"Sell is awreit," he interrupted with some relief. "No harm is done. It's true that when my wife worked here I got used to helping her, and it's true that you don't need the same kind of help. I'll try to remember. But," he went on, "you should remember to take care. You're not frail, but that doesn't mean you can't get hurt if you lift heavy things or don't take *gut* care climbing ladders."

Lilah nodded, looking a bit surprised. "I will be careful," she said. "I just… I really want to do a good job."

"You are doing a good job."

"I came here that day to ask for you to sell my quilts."

Eben tensed, but she went on quickly. "I didn't expect you to hire me to work in the store. It's not something I am too good at, but I'm thankful for the opportunity, so I want to pull my weight. And then, even after all I said—" she darted him a quick glance "—you know, about not liking you so much, you not only hired me, but you fixed my scooter without me even asking."

"The fix was simple enough."

"That depends on how you look at it," she said. "I couldn't figure out how to fix it myself, and it saved me having to take it to my brother Amos, who has more to do than time in the day. It's hard on my brothers sometimes. They've families to look after, and I hate to trouble them. But too often I have to."

"I'm sure they don't mind."

"I didn't say they minded. I said I hated to trouble them. I don't want to be a burden." She spoke matter-of-factly. "So to me, fixing the scooter was a very kind thing to do, and I appreciate it."

"Well, you bringing me lunch is kind, too."

She shrugged. "That's nothing."

He didn't argue, but it wasn't nothing to him. He'd begun to look forward to the tasty lunches she brought along for him most days.

He'd been a little thrown when she'd handed him the sandwiches and cookies that first day. And, honestly, a little suspicious. Women had brought him food before. Usually that meant they were trying to show him what good cooks they were and what fine wives they would make.

For that reason, he had a policy of politely refusing food when offered it. That saved time and trouble in the long run, he'd discovered. Anyway, he was used to feeding himself because Rose had never done much cooking.

He hadn't thought Lilah was trying to win him over like those other women, but it was a little odd, her bringing him food out of the blue like that. Especially since she'd made it clear he wasn't her favorite person. That was why he'd carried it back to the yard outside the store to double-check.

He'd been relieved to discover that Lilah was simply being... Lilah. She had too much food, and in her eyes, he had too little, so she'd shared. No other motive than decency and a sensible desire not to see good food go to waste.

That he could understand. And it meant he could eat the food without worrying about it giving a wrong impression.

And he'd been happy to fix her scooter. But he could see her point as well. Of course, a woman like Lilah, hardworking and a bit strong-minded, would hate being a bother to busy men with their own wives and *kinder* to tend to.

It was assumed, though, that such men would look after an unmarried sister. All men were expected to share in the care of any woman who was unmarried or a widow in the community. But of course, family took care of family first. The Plain community was always ready to help if needed, but folks looked after their own if they could. And since Lilah obviously felt she could rely on her *bruders*' help when she needed it, her family was doing their job well.

"I'm going to go sweep the sidewalk," Lilah was saying now. She'd taken over that job on her second day. "You can settle up the money."

She went in search of the broom, and he watched her go.

He had two unmarried *aents*, his father's sisters, neither living too close by. They were well looked after by family, and he saw them mainly at weddings and funerals. As a boy, he'd never questioned their unmarried state, and neither—as far as he knew—had anybody else.

He'd never have put Lilah in the same category. Why, he

wondered, had she never married? He searched his memory, but he never could remember her stepping out with any fellow. Of course, in Amish communities, sometimes you didn't know until the marriage was announced at church services, but often you could guess who was courting who.

Best he knew, Lilah hadn't been interested in any of the local boys. Except maybe Eben himself, he remembered uncomfortably. But he'd only had eyes for Rose back then.

Now, he thought, maybe, if he hadn't known Rose, he might have asked Lilah to ride home with him from a singing or two.

As he popped open the cash register and began counting out the money, a smile tickled around his lips.

Him courting Lilah Troyer. What an idea! Of course, it would never have worked out. The two of them would likely have ended up in an argument before the horse was three steps down the road.

But one thing was certain sure. That would have been a buggy ride to remember.

Two days later, Lilah pretended to focus on the conversation she was having with an elderly *Englisch* lady regarding whether or not the Amish cookbook she was considering would make a good bridal shower gift for her great niece.

Lilah nodded at the right times as the woman talked about how much better old-fashioned recipes were. But really, she was watching the foster boy, Corey, out of the corner of her eye.

He and his sister, Bethany, had come in about ten minutes ago on their own. They looked just as grubby as they had before, and the little girl's hair badly needed combing—and from the look of it, a good washing, too. Lilah suspected that the foster parents were doing some shopping and had decided to use Miller's General Store for free childcare.

She was sure Eben wouldn't mind. He was softhearted when it came to children. She didn't mind, either. These two young ones obviously needed all the kindness they could get. However, another problem was brewing.

Lilah shifted her position slightly so she could see around the shelf where Corey was standing. Today, he'd left Bethany to her own devices over in the toy area, while he looked over an array of pocketknives, temptingly arranged on a velvet cloth under a glass case.

That in itself wasn't so unusual. Lilah had noticed that it was a popular spot for boys his age. They often hovered there, looking longingly at the knives, which weren't cheap. Since they weren't particularly safe either, they were kept locked up.

Most of the time.

Eben had unlocked the case half an hour ago so that a man could make a purchase. Today had been busy, and he'd forgotten to lock it.

Corey had his eye on one those knives. Lilah was certain of it. Several of her brothers had really liked cookies hot out of the oven, and she'd learned the signs when one of them was about to go missing.

She'd also learned how to watch without letting on that she was watching, so she saw the minute he lifted up the lid of the glass case and snatched the closest knife. She had to give him credit. He was nimble-fingered. If she hadn't been keeping such a close eye, she'd never have noticed.

But she had. And this time, she intended to do something about it.

"Excuse me," she murmured, interrupting the lady in the

middle of a lengthy description of a casserole she'd once had at a friend's house.

Lilah strode purposefully in Corey's direction, and the boy's eyes widened in alarm.

"Come on, Bethany," he muttered. "We'd better go."

His sister had been playing with the wooden animals, making them talk softly to each other as she moved them about the shelf. She looked up at her brother with surprise.

"Why? Momma Karen said we were supposed to stay here until they came back."

"Yeah, well, we can wait outside." The boy grabbed his sister's arm and tugged her toward the door.

He was quick, but he wasn't quite quick enough. Lilah scooted in front of him and held out her hand, eyebrows raised.

She'd hoped that would be all it took, but Corey avoided her eyes and tried to sidestep her. She moved between him and the door, flexed her fingers and fixed him with a stern eye.

"I believe you've got something in your pocket that doesn't belong to you. Either hand it over or take it to the counter to pay for it."

The boy looked scared, but he scowled and refused to back down. "I don't know what you're talking about, lady. My sister and I need to go. Our parents are waiting for us."

That was a fib, and Lilah would have figured it out even if she hadn't known that those foster parents weren't the sort to wait on any children. Bethany was looking up at her brother wide-eyed, obviously confused.

"You know, it'll be much easier for everybody if you just hand over that pocketknife," she told him flatly. "You should be ashamed of yourself. The man who owns this store works very hard, and it's wrong of you to steal from him. He saw you take that cat the other day, but he didn't say anything. He didn't want to shame you, and this is how you repay his kindness? By stealing something else from him?"

"Corey!" Bethany tugged hard on her brother's arm, her eyes wide. "Are we in trouble?"

"You aren't, but your brother's about to be," Lilah told the little girl. Then she turned her attention back to the boy. "But it can all be fixed if you'll just hand over that knife."

"Lilah?" Suddenly, Eben appeared at her side. "What's going on here?"

She'd thought he was too busy at the counter to notice what was going on. She glanced over her shoulder to see an irritated line of customers waiting. He'd left them to come over and deal with this.

"This young man is trying to steal a pocketknife from you."

"Is that so?" Eben lifted an eyebrow.

"No, it ain't," Corey denied hotly, but wouldn't look Eben in the eye. He held out his empty hands, palms up. "See? I ain't stealing nothing. Me and my sister were just leaving, and this lady came up and stopped us."

"It's in his jeans pocket," Lilah said. "I saw him take it." When Eben hesitated, she added impatiently, "Go look in the case yourself if you don't believe me. You'll see. The one with the red handle is missing."

Eben kept his eye on Corey's flushed face. "If I go there and look, will there be a knife missing?"

Corey's mouth trembled, but he shrugged his thin shoulders defiantly. "How should I know? If there is, it's nothing to do with me."

For a second, Eben didn't speak. But then, to Lilah's astonishment, he nodded and stepped back. "Go on, then," he said. "And have a nice afternoon."

Corey's freckled face held a mixture of surprise and guilt, but it took him only a couple of seconds to recover his wits. He pulled Bethany quickly out the door and was gone.

Lilah put her hands on her hips. "Eben—" she started indignantly.

That was as far as she got. He shook his head.

"We'll not discuss it now. We've both got work to do."

He spoke in a low voice but in a tone that brooked no argument.

"Fine," Lilah said shortly. Then she turned on her heel and stalked away.

She fumed the rest of the afternoon as she helped customers and bagged up purchases at the counter. Even though she was often working at Eben's elbow, they barely spoke.

She did notice him go over and lock up the knife case as soon as he had a spare moment, and she felt a tiny flush of satisfaction. Now he'd see that the knife was missing, and he'd know she was telling the truth.

But his expression didn't change at all. He simply locked the case and returned to wait on more customers behind the counter.

It was a busy afternoon, and it was almost half an hour past closing time before the final customer left the shop. Eben locked the door, sighed deeply and then turned to face her.

"Go on," he said, his expression weary. "You've been simmering like a pot on a hot stove all afternoon. Say what you're thinking and get it out of your system."

"That boy stole the knife," she stated flatly.

"I know."

"You should have believed me."

"I did."

"I was telling the truth, and—" She paused. "You did? But you let him get away with it."

"Ja."

"Why?"

He sighed again and ran a hand through his hair. "For the same reason we let him take that cat. Because it's plain enough that he has a hard life. That hasn't changed, so I saw no reason to change how I responded to him."

Lilah opened her mouth to answer, then shut it with a snap. She pressed her lips together, and not trusting herself to say anything else, she simply nodded and turned away to complete the tasks she was responsible for.

She and Eben worked side by side for the next fifteen minutes. Then, when she'd finished, she went to the storeroom to collect her belongings.

In spite of her frustration, she surveyed the space with some satisfaction. It looked so much better than it had the first day she'd come. Smelled better, too. Nice and fresh and lemony from the polish she'd used on the floor. The shelves were organized neatly. It wasn't so nice as the front of the store, of course, but seeing the evidence of her hard work gave her a happy feeling of accomplishment.

Although, today that feeling was smudged a bit by irritation—and worry. Eben was too softhearted. She felt sorry for the children, too, but it shouldn't be allowed to continue. She might not be the one who tallied up the sales at the end of the day, but she could do math enough in her head to know that the profits weren't high enough that he could afford for people to steal from him regularly.

And besides—

"You might as well say it."

Lilah jumped and whirled around.

"Eben! You gave me a fright. Don't sneak up on me like that!"

"I was not sneaking. You were just too busy giving me a talking-to in your head to notice where I was." The wry amusement in his voice annoyed her a bit.

This wasn't funny. She turned her back to him and slid her empty lunch cooler off the shelf.

"I'm trying very hard to hold my tongue," she pointed out tartly. "But you're not making it easy."

"You can say your piece if you want."

"Why should I?" She whirled around to face him. "It won't change anything, will it? But I will say this much. Letting that little boy steal from you not once but twice—that was a mistake."

"My mistake to make," he pointed out reasonably.

"Well, maybe so, but if this store goes out of business because of such foolishness, I'll lose a job I need. And that's not even the worst of it."

He sighed and crossed his arms in front of his chest. "Let's hear it."

Lilah hesitated, but it had been a long day, and she was tired—and he was asking for it.

"Fine. It was one thing to let it go that first time. I did the same, as you know. But this time was different. He wasn't stealing something for his little sister. He was stealing for himself. I've a good bit less patience for that. And you said yourself that the boy hadn't anybody to teach him to have a good character, ain't so?"

He nodded, frowning.

"Well, you're doing that child no favors letting him practice his thievery in your store. Better you should hold him accountable. Sooner or later, he'll steal from someone who's not so kindhearted as you. Then what'll happen to him? Now, I'm going home. I'll see you tomorrow morning."

With that, she banged through the back door and hurried to collect her scooter. As she wheeled it through the wooden gate toward the sidewalk out front, her heart beat a hard rhythm in her chest.

Because she'd noticed Eben hadn't responded to her promise to see her tomorrow. And she knew better than most that while folks might say they wanted you to speak your mind, they rarely liked it when you did.

She'd just gotten herself fired, certain sure.

Chapter Six

Eben pulled into Susie Raber's yard an hour later and set the brake on his buggy.

And sighed.

He didn't want to have this conversation, but he didn't think it wise to put it off. When a man was wrong, it was best to get the apologies out of the way fast.

That didn't mean it was easy.

As he walked across the yard, he tried to think of the best way to say what he needed to say. He was so lost in his own thoughts that he was startled when the back door creaked open in front of him. He looked up to find Susie Raber studying him.

The widow's pleasant face was carefully serious, but there was a twinkle in her eye that made his toes crinkle in his boots. His *mamm* had looked much the same way when he'd gotten himself into trouble as a boy.

"Well, Eben," Susie said mildly. "It's a nice surprise to see you."

She didn't sound so very surprised at all, which made him wonder what exactly Lilah had told her when she'd gotten home from work.

"I need to talk to Lilah. About work," he added hastily, just so there'd be no misunderstandings.

Susie didn't blink. "She's in the living room, sewing a bit before supper time. I'm baking some bread. It's a new recipe, so I need to keep a close eye on the loaves I have in the oven while I'm readying the next batch of dough. I can't stop to visit, I'm afraid. As it is, I'll likely be baking until bedtime. But you can go on through." She nodded toward the open doorway leading out of the kitchen.

"Denki," Eben muttered as he wiped his boots and walked through the kitchen. It smelled strongly of yeasty bread, and he was reminded of his mother again.

And that he'd not eaten since lunch.

He stopped in the living room doorway. Lilah was seated in a rocker, a puddle of fabric in her lap. She was piecing together a small quilt top—a baby quilt, maybe. She must have heard him come in because she'd stuck her needle in the fabric, marking her stopping place. She looked up at him, her face pale and tense.

She certain sure didn't look very happy to see him. He didn't suppose he could blame her for that. He tried to collect his thoughts, but as usual, Lilah was quicker than he was.

"Hello, Eben." She rose to her feet. "I can guess why you're here, and I can't say I'm surprised to see you." She gave the pieced top a shake and began folding it carefully, keeping her gaze away from his.

Eben glanced over his shoulder into the kitchen, where Susie was leaning over to peek into the oven. She seemed absorbed in her baking, but was close enough that she could easily overhear every word they said. He'd come here prepared to make his apology to Lilah. He hadn't counted on having Susie listening in.

Somehow that made him feel even more awkward. He cleared his throat. "I've…uh…something to say to you."

"Oh, *ja*. I'm sure you do," Lilah murmured.

He blinked, momentarily thrown off balance. While he'd come here to make amends, best he could, it felt a little insulting that Lilah would be so confident of it.

He took a step forward to get a better look at her face. That worry pucker was creasing her forehead again, and if he didn't know better, he'd have thought Lilah was close to tears.

That made no sense at all.

"What exactly do you think I've come out here to say, Lilah?"

"That I'm fired, of course, for spouting off like I did. I've been expecting it, but I thought you'd wait until tomorrow morning. Although…" She appeared to reconsider. "I suppose it's kinder for you to come out here and save me the trip in to town. Thank you for that. Did you bring my last paycheck?"

"I did not. Because," he went on quickly, "I didn't come here to fire you."

"What?" Now Lilah looked up at him, her eyes wide. They regarded each other for a second. "Why did you come, then?"

There was a clatter of pans in the kitchen, reminding him of Susie just behind him, no doubt hearing every word spoken. He thought fast. An idea occurred to him.

"I'd like to ask you for a favor."

"A favor?" The worry pucker deepened. "What sort of favor?"

"I'm riding out to the Fishers to collect some items for the store. They're the ones who make the little carved animals and several other things I carry, and they've sent word that my last order is ready to pick up. They have some new items they want me to consider, too, things I might want to stock. I'd like for you to look over them and tell me which you think might be the best choices."

"I see," Lilah said, although she looked bewildered. "You really want my opinion?"

"That's right."

"Why?"

The question was blunt and direct and honest—much like Lilah herself. Eben felt a smile tickling the corners of his lips.

It was strange how often that was happening these days. Lilah didn't mean to be funny, of course, but she often was, and he just couldn't help grinning at her.

"You're a woman, ain't so? So are most of my customers. I'd like you to tell me what women would be most likely to buy."

He was pleased with himself for thinking that reason up so fast. It was true, too.

But as usual, Lilah wasn't so easily satisfied. "I'm not an *Englisch* woman, though, and I'd be unlikely to buy the things you carry. I'm not so sure I know much about what they'll like best." She tilted her head and considered. "But I suppose I could make a guess. If you really want me to."

He felt a wash of relief. "I do. *Denki*. I'll not keep you out late. It's only a twenty-minute buggy ride there, and they're real good about having the order packed up and ready for me."

She nodded. "I'll get my bonnet."

When they walked into the kitchen, Susie was carving off thick slices of fresh bread and slathering them with butter.

"Here. You can take these with you and eat them on the ride over to the Fishers. That should tide you over until supper."

So, as he'd suspected, she had been listening. As he accepted the snack with thanks, Eben felt doubly glad that he'd managed to talk Lilah into this errand. There'd be plenty of time to apologize during the buggy ride and no worry about anybody overhearing.

Of course, if he knew women—and he did because he had two sisters—Lilah would be telling Susie all about their conversation later this evening. But that was all right by him, so long as he didn't have to say his piece in front of an audience.

Once outside, he walked her around to the side of the buggy and offered his hand. She halted for a second, looking surprised, and he realized she'd expected to hoist herself into the buggy without any assistance.

He felt a little embarrassed. He'd always helped Rose, of course, and he hadn't driven a woman anywhere since... in a long while.

But then Lilah placed her hand in his and said simply, "*Denki*, Eben."

He should have answered her, but he didn't. He was too flustered—both by his unthinking action and by the feel of her fingers pressing against his palm. Her hand felt strong and steady and warm, and unlike Rose, she boosted herself into her seat with no trouble at all.

He settled himself in the buggy beside her, feeling awkward. With some relief, he focused on the familiar tasks of releasing the brake and clucking to Blaze. Soon they were on the two-lane road, clopping briskly toward the Fishers' farm.

"So," Lilah said after a second, "are you going to tell me what this is really about?"

He glanced at her, surprised. "How do you know it's not exactly what I said?"

She lifted an eyebrow.

"It might be, I suppose, but you've never asked my opinion about anything at the store before. Although," she added under her breath, "if you did, I'd have some things to say. And you've known you were making this trip for a while, I expect, and you're not the sort of man who waits until the last minute to ask a favor. If you'd wanted me along, you'd have asked me well before now." She shifted on the seat and smoothed her skirt.

He considered her words. She wasn't wrong.

"So," she went on, giving her dress one last tug. "What's this really about? Something to do with what happened at the store this afternoon? I'm sorry about what I said. It wasn't very respectful to speak to a boss that way. I did try to keep hold of my tongue. I really did. I just couldn't seem to manage it."

Rueful sincerity rang in her tone, and Eben found himself fighting a smile again. He firmed his mouth and slapped the reins on the horse's back. Best to get this over with.

"It wasn't about what you said. It was about what *I* said. Or more like what I didn't say." He took a breath. "You were right, and I was wrong. I shouldn't keep allowing Corey to steal from me."

If he'd expected a modest protest—or even any surprise—he'd have been disappointed. She didn't say a word.

He sneaked a glance at her and found her looking back at him calmly.

"Well, you didn't have to make a special trip to tell me so," she said. "I knew that much already."

He couldn't help it. He barked a laugh so loud that one of Blaze's ears swiveled backward in alarm. Lilah was one of a kind, for certain sure.

"I wanted to apologize to you. It's true that if Corey's

allowed to take things from my store without paying, I'm encouraging him to have a bad character. The fact that I feel sorry for him doesn't excuse his behavior. And the fact that he has nobody else to teach him right from wrong just means it's all the more important that somebody step up to do it."

Lilah was nodding. "Not a pleasant job," she said. "And not yours to do. But as you say, it does seem that nobody else cares about the boy or his sister." She clucked her tongue sadly. *"'Sis en aylend."*

"Ja, you are right. It is a very sad situation. But I was only making it worse."

Lilah tilted her head thoughtfully. "Maybe so. But I don't see as how you owe me any apology. It was your pocket-knife he stole, so the theft cost me nothing."

"But I did not uphold you in front of him, even though you were right."

She shrugged. "It's your store. I just work there. It's my job to do as you say." She slanted him a glance. "As you've pointed out more than once."

She was joking with him. He could hear it in her voice, and his heart lifted a notch. The hard part was over now.

"True." He quirked an eyebrow at her. "I wasn't so sure you remembered that."

She laughed then, a short, bubbly sound that made him lose control of the smile he'd been fighting. They rode along in a companionable silence for a few minutes, both smiling out at the sweet, summery world.

It was a nice evening. Now that it was June, the day-light lasted a good long while, but the heat of the day had spent itself, and a cool breeze blew out of the woods lining the little road, bringing the scent of pines, fresh grass and cows. There wasn't much traffic, so it was a peaceful drive.

He'd made it lots of times, and he'd always enjoyed it well enough. But now, with Lilah sitting beside him, looking at the passing scenery with an alert interest, it seemed even more pleasant than usual.

It was nice to have company, he thought. Especially the company of a woman. Of course, there'd been plenty of women who'd have accepted an invitation from him for a buggy ride, likely enough. But that sort of invitation came with expectations.

With Lilah, he'd no worries about such things. He was free to simply enjoy her company and the sweetness of the summer afternoon.

"You know," Lilah said thoughtfully. "I might have a word with the Fishers about those little animals while we're out there. You could sell a sight more of them if the price was lower."

"Ah…" It suddenly occurred to Eben that maybe this drive with Lilah wouldn't turn out to be so trouble-free after all. Given her blunt-spoken ways, she was likely to insult one of his best suppliers.

But even as he floundered for the best way to discourage her from her latest idea, he once again, for some reason, found himself fighting a smile.

The Fishers' farm was a swarm of busy activity. Children of various ages were everywhere, and Lilah felt a surge of wistful happiness as they rolled into the drive.

Ach, Ruth Fisher was a blessed woman, certain sure.

"I'll tend to the horse," a boy offered as soon as Eben had pulled to a stop. The little fellow was only about ten, but a pair of calm, resolute eyes looked out from underneath his blond bangs. Eben's horse would be in capable hands.

Eben must have felt the same because he didn't hesitate.

"*Denki*, Aaron," he said. "I won't be long. I just need to talk to your *daed* a minute. Is he in the workshop?"

"*Ja*, him and *mamm* both." The boy nodded toward a low stone building a small distance from the house and barn. Probably once a dairy barn, Lilah supposed. A lot of Amish businessmen were turning such places into workshops for the cottage industries that put food on their tables.

And the Fishers would need plenty of food to feed their growing family. They had nine children so far. Lilah felt bad about bringing up the price of the animals.

But, if she could find a polite way to do it, she would. Eben needed to make a profit, too. Those carvings were well-done and cute, but the prices were much too high. She'd dusted that shelf several times since coming to work at Miller's General Store, and so far the only animal that had left the store was the one that had been smuggled out in Corey's pocket.

Eben reached for the small paper sack that had been sitting between them on the ride over before climbing out of the buggy. She jumped out herself before he could make it around to the side to help her.

That had been a little awkward back at the house. She wasn't used to being helped into buggies—although it was real nice and polite to do.

He waited for her as Aaron took charge of the horse. "It's this way."

Eben, she soon discovered, was a well-known visitor. As he strode toward the low-roofed building, a crowd of little Fishers rushed toward him. They flocked from the neat-rowed garden and the barn, calling to one another in *Deutsch* as they ran.

"It's Eben! Eben's here!"

They halted around him in a hopeful circle, the girls'

bare feet and hands grubby from kneeling in the garden soil, the boys with sprigs of hay caught in their hair.

Eben smiled down at the *kinder*, that same gentle light in his eyes that she'd first noticed in the store.

"This is a fine welcome for a weary man," he said. "You know Lilah?"

Of course, they did. Everyone in their small Plain community knew each other, at least a little.

She smiled. "Hello. It's *gut* to see you."

Shy smiles responded, accompanied by some nods and some murmured hellos. Then the children's eyes shifted back to Eben. There was an expectant silence.

Eben returned their gazes innocently, a twinkle in his eye. "I've *komm* to see your parents. Aaron said they're in the workshop."

Glances were exchanged. A little girl who looked to be maybe eight or nine spoke up.

"*Ja*, they are finishing up some painting before supper. We are weeding the garden and tending to the animals."

"Ah," Eben said sagely. "That sounds like hungry work."

Lots of earnest nods. The children's eyes focused on the paper bag Eben carried in one hand.

"I'm sure you're glad supper's coming on so soon, then," Eben said, taking a step forward. The children's faces fell, and they backed up a step, clearing the path to the workshop.

"Mach's gut," several murmured politely as they turned sadly back to their chores.

"All right." Eben chuckled. "If you promise not to eat it until after your dinner." He began pulling sticks of candy from his bag.

The children's eyes brightened, and they laughed as they gratefully accepted the treats. The oldest girl carefully collected them from the smaller children. "I'll put these in the kitchen for safekeeping," she said. "You can have them once the dishes are done. *Denki*, Eben."

As the children scampered back to their work, Lilah slanted a glance up at Eben. "Do you bring them candy every time you come?"

He shrugged. "It's a small enough thing to do, and it makes them happy," he said gruffly.

"It certainly seemed to. Likely, in a big family like this there's little money for store-bought treats, so I expect it's extra special for them."

He lifted an eyebrow. "No fuss, then, about me giving away free candy?"

"Of course not."

"But you're planning to fuss about the price of the carvings, ain't so?"

She frowned. "Not fuss, no. Just ask a question or two, that's all." An idea occurred to her, and she flushed. "Unless you don't want me to say anything. As you keep pointing out, it's your store, not mine. I didn't think... The prices really are too high," she murmured softly—they were getting very close to the shop now, and she didn't want to be overheard. "And they'd sell a good many more, I think, if it could be lowered, which would be good for you and them both. But if you'd rather I didn't say anything—"

Before she could finish, the workshop door opened, and a pleasant-faced blonde woman stood in the doorway, holding a tiny girl in her arms.

Ruth Fisher smiled warmly at her visitors. "Eben! And Lilah. Come in! It's so nice to see you both, especially you, Lilah. I'd heard you were working in Eben's store now."

Eben went in first, and as Lilah followed, Ruth winked at her. Lilah blinked, unsure what that was supposed to mean.

Then she put it out of her mind. The Fishers' workshop was too full of interesting things to be distracted by winks.

The long, narrow space had been converted to a work area, with simple wooden tables and plain cupboards for supplies. The open shelves lining the walls were crammed with finished products, and the sharp tang of fresh paint hung heavily in the air.

"Ruth, would you show Lilah the newer things you'd like me to consider while Mark and I double-check this order? I want her opinion about which items are likeliest to sell to my women customers."

"Sure," Ruth said. "We've put the newer items all together, so they'll be easier for you to look over."

Lilah followed Ruth to a corner of the building where an assortment of crafts were arranged on a table.

"Mark's made these tops." Ruth picked up a polished wooden top and gave it a deft spin. It teetered merrily along the crowded table, bumping gently into other items.

Lilah nodded her approval. "*Ja*, children will like that. Mothers and grandmothers will buy them, for sure."

"*Gut!* We've only made a few so far, but we can have lots more made before Eben comes out for the next order. How many do you think he'd want?"

"That depends," Lilah said cautiously. "What'll you sell them to the store for?"

Ruth looked surprised and darted a quick look in Eben's direction. He and her husband were busy going through boxes, checking off the packed items from a handwritten list. "I—I'm not so sure." Obviously she wasn't prepared to talk about the prices, so Lilah smiled.

"That's all right. But I wouldn't want you to waste your time, so I can tell you about what we could sell these for." She thought a second and quoted a price. "And if you haven't made many of them yet, I'd add some colored stripes. The varnish is pretty, but children like bright colors."

Ruth blinked at her. "That sounds like a *gut* idea."

"So? What else do you have?"

The two women went through the samples one by one. Most of them would do well for the store, Lilah thought, so by the end of it, Ruth was smiling happily.

Lilah glanced at a nearby shelf, crowded with faceless dolls wearing Plain clothing and a neat pile of folded aprons.

"What about this shelf? I haven't seen any of these items in the store. Why weren't they on the table?"

"Oh!" Ruth lowered her voice. "Eben has never been interested in any of our fabric items. I offered a few to him before, but he always turned them down."

"Have you offered the things on this shelf?"

"*Nee*, not those exactly, but—"

"Add them in," Lilah said quickly. Maybe Eben would fuss, but she'd cross that bridge when she came to it. She knew these items would sell quick and for a real *gut* price. "The aprons, and a few of those dollies there, too." Those would be a nice touch for the toy shelf, and she'd had several women asking about dolls like that. "If," she added belatedly, "they won't be too expensive."

"Oh, no." Ruth's face lit up. "I can make these things for cheap. I use scraps, and my *dochders* help me with the sewing. Only the older girls," she added hastily. "And I always check to make sure they are doing a *gut* job."

"I can see that you do. Better have a good many ready because if we set a fair price, I think these will fly off the shelves."

Ruth nodded happily. "I will."

Although Lilah hated to spoil the mood, maybe it was a *gut* time to bring up the pricing of the animals. She walked to the shelf where several of the carvings were lined up. She ran a finger across the top of a little donkey and came away with a smudge of dust.

Ruth looked embarrassed. "Those have been sitting awhile," she said apologetically. "Eben hasn't ordered any lately."

"Ja," Lilah said carefully. "They aren't good sellers because you've got them priced too high. I know they take time, and they're real well made. But isn't there any way you can make them cheaper?"

She'd worried that Ruth might be offended by the question, but the other woman only cocked her head and considered the array of animals thoughtfully. "I don't know," she murmured. "Some of them take a good amount of time to make. Time we could spend on other projects. That accounts for the pricing."

The two women studied the shelf in silence for a second or two. Then an idea occurred to Lilah.

"Some of them take time," she repeated. "But not all of them, ain't so? Some are simpler than others."

"That's right."

"Separate them," Lilah ordered briskly. "Into the ones that take the most time and the ones that are the quickest to make. Let's see how they divide up."

She watched as the other woman moved the animals around, putting some on one side and some on the other. Finally, when she had them all divided, she looked back at Lilah.

"There. That's the best I can do. So?"

"So talk to your *mann* and see what's the best price he can give us on the simpler ones. There's no reason why all of them should be priced the same. We'll give a better deal on the ones that don't take so long to make, and we'll stock in more of those, maybe. But some of the pricier ones, too, because there'll be folks who'll want a set. And that's another idea! Try grouping some together, mixing a couple of the cheaper ones with an expensive one, packaged up nice. People will be likelier to pay more that way, I think."

Ruth was nodding. "Those are *schmaert* ideas!"

"What ideas?" Eben had walked within earshot, and he and Mark looked at them curiously. Lilah was glad that Ruth took the lead, enthusiastically explaining the ideas about pricing the animals differently.

The two men looked at each other for a second. Then Eben nodded slowly.

"I think that might work real well. And did you decide which of the new items we should stock, Lilah?"

"I did, *ja*. Or I think I did. Do you want to—"

"Nee," Eben interrupted. "I trust your judgment in this. Go ahead and make up our next order with the things she liked. You know how many I usually order when we're trying something new. Let me know when they're ready to pick up, and I'll come back out to get them. Now, let's get these boxes loaded into the back of the buggy, Mark. I need to be getting back, and your *kinder* will be wanting their suppers soon."

"They will—if they haven't already filled their stomachs with your candy," Ruth laughed.

The two men each hefted up a box and began to walk toward the buggy. When Lilah started to follow, Ruth tugged at her sleeve.

"Denki, Lilah," she said. "This extra work will make a nice difference for us. Eben's always been kind, but he's never placed such a big order before." The woman's green eyes twinkled. "I hope you'll handle all the ordering from here on."

"That would be fun," Lilah admitted. She'd enjoyed this even more than she'd expected. "But of course, he only brought me along to get a woman's opinion. Mostly he has me cleaning and restocking the shelves, and that keeps me plenty busy."

"Well, anybody could do such simple jobs," Ruth pointed out reasonably as they walked across the yard to Eben's waiting buggy. "Even a child could be trained for those. And it would free you up to do more of this sort of thing."

Lilah glanced over to the yard pump, where three of the Fisher girls were washing their dirty hands and feet before going inside. Then she considered the garden, green and lush in the late afternoon sunshine, not a weed to be seen.

Ruth was right. Children handled simple jobs very well. And it was *gut* training for both their bodies and their minds.

Their characters, too.

An idea suddenly occurred to her. She turned it over in her mind as they said their goodbyes. By the time she and Eben were back in the buggy, she'd come to a decision. She knew exactly what needed to be done.

Now she just had to convince Eben to agree with her.

Chapter Seven

To Eben's surprise, Lilah didn't start talking about prices and products the minute he pointed the buggy back toward Susie's home. Instead, she held her tongue and looked thoughtful as they rode along in a peaceful silence.

He toyed with the idea of making some small talk—in his experience, women tended to expect that. But Lilah seemed content, and for his part, he was enjoying the quiet.

Not that he'd have minded if she'd wanted to talk. Not at all. Lilah might be a little too plainspoken for some, but at least she was never boring.

The truth was, he'd enjoyed this errand—and Lilah's company—a good deal more than he'd expected to.

He pondered that surprising fact as Blaze jogged down the road, the crisp clopping of the gelding's hooves mingling with the sounds of frogs and crickets tuning their voices up for the evening.

Ja, he decided, he'd enjoyed this afternoon very much, once he'd gotten the apology out of the way. Lilah had done well out at the Fishers'. His worries that she might be too blunt with her opinions and cause hard feelings had come to nothing. Instead, she'd been kind, polite and pleasant. She'd handled the decisions about the new stock well, too.

In fact, it had been a relief to let Lilah deal with all that while he double-checked the packed order with Mark. He'd only suggested the task as a way to get her alone so he could apologize, but he had to admit, it had worked out nicely.

He'd always had to make all the decisions relating to the store—and everything else—himself. Rose had been easily overwhelmed, so she'd been content to leave most everything in his hands. For years, he'd managed the store, their household and pretty much all their other responsibilities, even those that usually fell to an Amish wife.

That had been all right. He'd not minded.

But today, Lilah had stepped right up and taken charge of things as if she'd been born to do it. She'd not dithered about it, nor pestered him with questions. She'd even managed to deal with that sticky issue of the carved animal prices in a real *schmaert* way. Not bad, considering she'd never run a store herself.

Ja, Lilah might be a bit too outspoken at times, but she was a real bright and capable woman. And because of her help, some of the burden he'd carried for so long had slipped off his shoulders.

He was grateful for that.

"Denki," he said suddenly. "For helping me today. You did a *gut* job back there at the Fishers'."

Lilah jumped when he spoke, as if he'd jarred her out of her own thoughts. She smiled and shrugged.

"I only did what you'd asked, but you're welcome. I'm glad if I was some help."

"You were a good bit of help, and I appreciate it."

"I'm glad," she repeated. "I enjoyed it. The Fishers are a nice family." She paused, as if weighing her next words carefully. "I like the way they are bringing up their little ones."

Eben remembered the happy flock of young Fishers back at the farm, and a smile spread across his face. "You're right about that. They are smart, sweet children, and Mark and Ruth seem like real wise parents. Not," he added with a quick shrug, "that I know so much about such things, not being a parent myself."

"Well, me either," Lilah said. "But of course, we both of us had parents even if *Gott* in His wisdom didn't choose to give us children of our own, ain't so? So we do know a little something about it."

"I suppose so."

"You especially," she went on. "I've noticed from working in the store how good you are with little ones. I think you'd have made a real fine father."

Eben shifted uneasily on the buggy seat. He wasn't sure quite how to answer that. This wasn't a topic usually discussed, except maybe in the most intimate family relationships. Certainly not in a buggy between a man and a woman who only worked together.

But, as usual, Lilah spoke her mind without a trace of self-consciousness and seemed unbothered by the sensitive subject. So, after a second or two, he decided to be unbothered by it as well.

"I'd have liked to have children," he admitted. "If it had been *Gott*'s will." He'd never said that out loud to anybody, not even Rose, although he was sure she'd known it. But she'd blamed herself enough for their lack of family, and he hadn't wanted to add to her sorrow by talking about his own.

"I'd have liked a family, too," Lilah was saying. "But it seems the Lord had other plans for us. Maybe—"

She stopped short, and he shot her a curious look. One thing about Lilah, she usually wasn't too shy about sharing her thoughts, so it wondered him that she seemed hung up on whatever she wanted to say next.

"Maybe what?" he prompted finally.

"Well." She shifted in the buggy so she was half facing him. "I've been thinking about that little *Englisch* boy, Corey. He needs somebody in his life to teach him right from wrong. I think we can both agree on that."

He nodded cautiously. "*Ja*, that's so."

"Those people who're supposed to be looking after him don't seem to be doing such a great job, and of course, his own parents must not be able to help much, either. Otherwise he and his sister wouldn't be in foster care to start with."

"*Ja*," he said again. "That's a pity." He glanced sideways and found her looking at him intently. Even in the shadow of the buggy, he could read the determination on her face. "What?"

"I think you'd be real *gut* at that, Eben. At teaching a little boy like that how to behave and how to work hard and be honest. Just like Mark and Ruth are teaching their *kinder*. And if Corey could learn those things, it could change his life for the better, couldn't it?"

"I suppose it could. But what could I do? I'm not his *daed*, nor even his…" He had to search his memory for the words. "Foster parent. It's not my place to teach him anything."

"*Nee*, not as things stand now. But—"

"But what?"

"Well, what if he worked for you?"

"Worked for me?" He was so astonished he almost dropped the reins. "What are you talking about? He's a child."

"I know that," Lilah said. "Of course, a boy that age couldn't work for you officially. Not for pay or anything like that. But our children help their parents out all the time, ain't so? Just like we saw back at the Fishers'. The girls were weeding the garden, and the boys were working in the barn. Ruth told me the older girls help her with the sewing, too. That was the way it was in my house growing up. Yours, too, I'm guessing. We learned useful skills that way and to be dependable and responsible grown-ups, didn't we?"

"Well, yes, of course. But—Plain folks raise their children different from the *Englisch*." He shouldn't have to point that out. Surely she knew that as well as he did.

"Oh, I don't think they're so different, not the good ones. Anyway, this Corey seems to have no real parenting at all, good or otherwise. You could make a difference to that child, Eben Miller." She spoke with such conviction that it startled him.

He shook his head. "I still don't see how."

"I have an idea. We'll have to wait until he steals again, but when he does, we can suggest he help out a little at the store to pay for the theft instead of us calling the police over it."

"But I wouldn't call the police."

"Of course not, but he doesn't know that. Neither will those foster parents. I expect they'll be happy enough to have him occupied and out of their house for a few hours at a time." She nodded so emphatically that her bonnet slid a little. "Once he's at the store regularly, you can help him build up his character. It'll work. You wait and see."

Eben wasn't so sure about that, but since they were rolling into Susie's driveway, there wasn't any time for arguing. "He might not ever steal again," he said hopefully, but Lilah shook her head.

"Oh, *ja*, he will. He's gotten away with it twice now. It's just a matter of time."

"Hello, there!" Susie appeared at the back door, wiping

her hands with a dish towel. "You two are back just in time. I'm about to put supper on the table. Would you like to stay, Eben? I've baked two hens, so there's more than enough."

The scent of roasted chicken drifted from the glowing kitchen doorway, and his mouth watered. He hesitated. Usually he wasn't so tempted to accept dinner invitations. In fact, he'd refused so many since Rose's death that he rarely got them anymore, except from family.

But before he could decide how to answer, he caught sight of Lilah's face.

She was frowning at Susie, her eyes narrowed. She wasn't a bit happy about the idea of him staying for the meal, that was plain to see.

"I expect Eben needs to get home," she said. "He's been gone all the day, and I'm sure he has lots of things to tend to."

"*Denki*, Susie," he said politely. "But Lilah's right. I'd best be getting along. Thank you for coming with me, Lilah. You were a big help." He started to set the brake and get down to help her out of the buggy, but at the last minute he decided against it. Best he should stay where he was and let her manage on her own.

"You're welcome, Eben. I'll see you at work tomorrow." She spoke without looking at him, her attention focused on getting out of the buggy.

"*Mach's gut.*" As soon as she was clear, he clucked to Blaze and started off, leaving Lilah, Susie and the delicious smells behind him.

The road was still peaceful and the breeze pleasantly cool, but Eben's mood had deflated. It was a good thing, he reminded himself, that Lilah had no desire to spend extra time with him outside of work. After all, one of the reasons he'd hired her in the first place was because she'd no interest in him as a potential husband.

He was real thankful for that. Of course, he was. And, of course, he wanted things to stay just as they were. Everything was working out just fine.

But just now, as he pointed his buggy toward his empty house—and his equally empty pantry—he wasn't nearly as happy about all that as he should have been.

"You shouldn't have done that," Lilah fussed irritably.

When she'd walked into the kitchen, Susie had three places set at the table. The empty plate stared back at her reproachfully.

"What? Invited Eben? Why wouldn't I? It's only polite, since he was bound to be hungry by this time of day and after such a long drive, too. Plus, we know he's no *frau* at home to cook him a decent meal. It seemed a neighborly thing to do."

"Neighborly?" Lilah gathered up the extra plate and silverware and put them away in the cupboards. "You weren't being neighborly. You were playing matchmaker again."

Susie only chuckled as she settled herself at the table. "Well, what are you worried about? Even if I was, it's plain I'd be wasting my time. You made no secret of how you feel about Eben. You practically slapped his horse on the rear to get him out of here faster."

Lilah paused, one hand on the back of her own chair. Had she been rude? She hadn't meant to be. She'd just been very embarrassed.

"I didn't want him thinking I'd put you up to it." She pulled out the chair and slid into her place. "I need that job, and it's clear he's not interested in getting married again.

If he suspects you're trying to match the two of us up, he's likely to start looking for another helper in the store."

"Maybe." Susie sounded irritatingly unconvinced. "Then again, maybe a nice hot supper and some pleasant company would have been welcome. Welcome enough that he might have overlooked my matchmaking just this once." Before Lilah could argue, Susie bowed her head for the silent grace.

Lilah had no choice but to follow suit. It was hard, though, to focus on thanking *Gott* for the good food steaming in front of her. For one thing, she didn't much like the thought of Eben going home to no supper—or a pitiful one—and going by his lunches, he almost certainly was.

And for another, Susie didn't seem nearly disappointed enough. In the past, when one of her matchmaking schemes had failed, her friend had been downright indignant.

This resigned cheerfulness seemed suspicious.

"How were the Fishers?" Susie asked as soon as grace was over.

"They seemed very well," Lilah answered, grateful for the change of subject. The supper proceeded pleasantly as Lilah recounted the details of their errand. She added in her idea about Corey, inspired by the Fisher children, and Susie listened thoughtfully.

"I think that's a real *gut* idea," she said. "It's wrong, of course, to hope that the child steals again, but I almost do because I agree with you. That little boy could use some guidance, and Eben might very well be the making of him." She helped herself to another slice of chicken. "You know, that was a very Christian attitude for you to have."

Lilah had been stirring her green beans around on her plate, thinking uncomfortably about Eben going home to an empty table. She looked up, startled. "What?"

"Ruth Fisher's about your age, ain't so?" Susie said. "And

she's got a kind husband and a real nice home and house-ful of healthy children. I'm sure you'd like to have all those things yourself. I know I would. A good many women in our position might have left the Fishers feeling envious. Maybe they'd have been tempted to pick at some little fault they saw in Ruth or in her children. Instead, you admired her. And now you're taking that admiration and trying to turn it into a blessing. Because it will be a blessing, not only for that poor little *Englisch* boy, but for Eben himself, if it works out well."

Lilah shifted uncomfortably in her seat. She started to say that of course she wasn't envious of Ruth. But, she realized, that wouldn't be completely true. Maybe she was a little bit envious, although, of course, she should only be thankful that Ruth was so richly blessed.

"*Gott* calls different people to lead different lives," she said finally. "Mine is different from Ruth's, but I've plenty of reasons to be content with what I have. I have loving brothers and good friends, and one of them has given me a comfortable home to live in. Now I've a job that I enjoy, too. That's enough for me."

"A very wise attitude," Susie murmured. Then she began talking about the new breads she'd tried out that day and which ones she felt would work best in the bakery.

Lilah listened politely, but her mind lingered on Susie's remarks all through supper and the cleanup. She was still thinking on it as she went upstairs and prepared for bed.

She sat down in her white nightgown in the old wooden rocking chair in her room, close to the open window. A cool evening breeze ruffled the curtain, bringing in the scents of Susie's summer flowers. Lilah rocked gently, listening to the familiar sounds of Susie preparing for bed in her own room down the hall.

Lilah had never lived alone, although once she'd stayed home by herself for a weekend when Susie went out of town for a relative's wedding. It had all worked out fine, of course, but she remembered the echoing emptiness of the house with a shudder. That had been the first night she'd spent all alone, and she hadn't much liked it. No wonder, she'd thought at the time, that Susie was so eager to rent out her spare bedroom to other single women.

Ja, like she'd told Susie at supper, she had much to be thankful for. After all, Eben went home to an empty house every night. No one to have supper with, no one to talk over the day with. Only memories to keep him company.

It was surprising, she thought, that he wasn't interested in marrying again. As Susie had pointed out more than once, there were plenty of women who'd happily accept Eben Miller for a husband. He could easily have a family like the Fishers for himself. Women had no real choice in the matter, apart from refusing someone they didn't want to marry.

Of course, for her, even that had never happened. Nobody had ever shown any interest in marrying Lilah.

But a man like Eben? He had a choice.

Lilah suddenly realized—with a longing so fierce it surprised her—what choice she'd make, if she had the choosing. She'd have a family like Ruth Fisher's. A big, wonderful, loud family, with plenty of children to guide and to love, and a husband to fuss over and cook for and laugh with.

The rocking chair creaked to a stop, and Lilah sighed once, deeply.

Maybe she wasn't quite as content as she'd told Susie she was, after all.

Chapter Eight

The following Monday afternoon, Eben kept his head bowed as if he were looking at the copy of *The Budget* he'd spread over the counter. Really, he was watching Corey.

The boy had come in with his sister about thirty minutes ago. The foster parents hadn't stayed this time. Eben had heard them mention going down to the Yoders' restaurant again.

Eben didn't believe they were planning to buy more bulk groceries. He suspected that they were going there to eat and had simply decided not to take the children with them. Which, in Eben's mind, was a mean-spirited choice to make, especially given how hungry the young ones looked. And it probably explained why Corey had been lingering around the store's display of homemade candies.

In fact, he'd been doing more than just lingering.

By Eben's count, at least four of the small bags of fudge and caramels were now in Corey's jacket pockets. That jacket... Eben had sighed the minute he'd seen the child wearing it.

The worn-out denim jacket was proof that Lilah was right. Corey had come into the store planning to steal. The summer weather was far too warm for any sort of coat.

He wasn't the only one who'd noticed what the boy was

up to. Lilah was watching, too, although she was careful
to keep her distance. Like Eben, she pretended to be distracted by rearranging shelves and chatting with the other
customers.

But business was slow this afternoon, and soon the children were the only customers in the store. Corey crammed
another bag of sweets into his bulging pockets and looked
up. This time, Eben looked back, and the boy's expression
shifted into alarm.

"Come on, Bethany," he muttered. "We got to go."

"Where?" Bethany looked up at her brother, wide-eyed.
She had one of the little animals in her hands, a duck this
time. "We're s'posed to wait here until Momma Karen and
Wayne come back."

"We can wait outside just as well. They ain't gonna care."
He took the duck and placed it back in its spot. Then he
reached for his sister's hand, tugging her toward the door.

Bethany followed, her small face scrunched in confusion and unhappiness. "But why, Corey? I like looking at
the toys in here."

Eben rounded the counter. Before the children reached
the door, he stepped in front of them.

"Your brother wants to leave," he said gently, "because
he is trying to steal some sweets."

"I ain't neither!" Corey protested hotly. Before he could
say another word, Lilah, who'd walked briskly up to join
them, reached out and plucked a cellophane bag of chocolate drops from his pocket.

"What's this, then?"

Corey's face flushed red. "I was gonna pay for those. I
just forgot."

Eben turned around and flipped the sign on the door
to Closed. When Lilah lifted an eyebrow, he explained, "I

think we will close early today. This young man and I need to have a talk."

Corey's expression shifted again, this time to fear, but he puffed out his skinny chest. "I ain't got nothing to say to you."

"That's all right," Eben said mildly. "I have some things I'd like to say, though." He noticed how the boy had tucked his sister behind his own body, as if trying to protect her.

He sighed. There was good in this boy, anyone with eyes could see that. It only needed to be brought out.

"If you close up your store, you're gonna lose a lot of business over one little old bag of candy," the boy argued desperately.

And the child was smart, too—at least enough to make a good argument.

"True. But you have at least four more bags in your pockets," Eben pointed out.

Corey was looking more and more worried. "Fine. I'm sorry, all right? Here."

He took bag after bag out of his pockets, placing them on a nearby shelf. Five more cellophane sacks appeared, each tied with a little snip of ribbon.

"You missed one," Lilah remarked to Eben. When he glanced at her, her lips were twitching.

"Ja." The woman was a bad influence. Now she had him wanting to grin, too, and this was not a funny matter. "My eyes are not what they used to be."

"There," Corey said. "I gave everything back. Now can we go?"

"Not this time. I'm sorry, but this is too important to let slide."

"It's just candy." The boy was shaking now. "They don't cost hardly nothing. Three dollars apiece, these small ones.

Besides, you got lots more of 'em, and all this other stuff in the store. Why do you even care if somebody takes a little bit?"

"About the candy? I don't." He squatted down now so he could look the boy in the face. "Honestly, if you'd have asked, I'd likely have given it to you. Especially since I figure you're probably pretty hungry." He paused. "Ain't so?"

The boy didn't answer, but Eben could see that he'd guessed correctly.

"The candy's not what's important. You are. You're more important than the stuff you're stealing, and you're more important than the business I'll lose closing my store up early to talk to you about it. *Gott* teaches us that stealing is a wrong thing to do, and it won't lead to anything good." Eben shook his head sorrowfully. "I don't like seeing you on such a path, and I want to help you get off it and onto a better one, if I can."

He had the boy's attention now. Corey stared up at him, his gray-green eyes wide.

"But why—" the boy started. Then he stopped.

"Why what?"

"Why do you even care what happens to me?" he whispered.

Eben looked up and met Lilah's eyes. This time, there was no amusement twinkling in them at all, only a shocked sorrow.

He felt the same, and it took him a few seconds before he could answer the boy's question.

"Because I do," he said quietly. "Because you're a human being loved by *Gott*, and because I think you might need a little help right now." He cleared his throat. "But you're old enough to make your own choices, I think. So I'll leave it up to you. You can go on out the door, if you like. There's a bench in front of the store where you can wait for your... folks to come get you. Or you and your sister can stay inside with me and Lilah here. We'll give you something to eat, and we'll have ourselves a little talk and figure this out. So?" He stood back up. "Which will it be?"

He watched as Corey weighed his options. Finally the boy looked down into his sister's face. "If I stay to talk with you, you'll give *both* of us something to eat?"

Eben's heart clenched. "I will."

Corey nodded. "Then I guess we'll stay."

In five minutes, with Lilah's help, he had the children settled at the storeroom table, paper towels in front of them laden with what food he could scrounge from his shelves. It wasn't much—some peanut butter crackers he'd kept handy for emergency lunches before Lilah came and some pretzels and candies. He wished he hadn't eaten both of the chicken sandwiches Lilah had brought him for lunch. That would be something nutritious for the children to eat. But he had eaten them, so they just had to make do with what they had.

The children certainly had no complaints. They dug into the simple food hungrily. Lilah and Eben exchanged glances as they ate. Lilah's eyes were full of sad compassion, and he noticed how she quietly replenished the snacks on the paper towels when they got low.

"So," Eben said after a few minutes. "We need to figure this out, Corey. You can't keep on stealing. That candy today was the third time, at least."

"Okay." Corey toyed with a pretzel. "I'll stop."

"That's good, but it doesn't pay Eben here for what you've already stolen," Lilah pointed out. "The candy's not so expensive, but that pocketknife you took was."

"I could bring it back."

"You could, *ja*. But he can't sell it now," Lilah pointed

out. "At least, not for the same price. It's not new anymore. And neither is the little cat you took."

Bethany was drinking some water from the bottle Lilah had given her. She choked in mid-gulp, her face stricken. Corey patted her on the back as she coughed.

"It's okay, Bethany," he said. "You can keep the cat. I'll fix this." He looked up at Eben. "What do I gotta do?"

Eben's and Lilah's eyes met, and she gave him a tiny nod. *Go ahead.*

"Well," Eben said slowly. "I have an idea that might work well for both of us."

He explained Lilah's idea that Corey could help out in the store for a few hours a week. First to pay for the things he'd already taken, and then in exchange for any little items he'd like to have. If, of course, his foster parents would agree to it.

"Oh, they ain't gonna care," Corey said immediately. "They don't care about nothing I do, as long as it's no trouble to them."

As if on cue, there was a knocking at the door. Eben tipped back his chair to see the children's foster parents peering in, looking annoyed.

"Looks like we can check with them right now." He got up and went to let them in.

They were irritated, more so when Corey admitted what was going on. And Eben couldn't help but notice that they smelled of onions and there was a drip of ketchup on Wayne's shirt front.

Just as he'd suspected. These two had been over at Yoder's enjoying a hamburger while their two foster kids went without. Indignation welled up in him, and he had to work to keep his tone civil.

After he'd outlined his plan, the two *Englischers* looked at each other.

"Better than him calling the police," Wayne muttered. "Not that the little troublemaker don't deserve it, but they report that kinda thing to the social workers. That'll cause problems for us, too." The man shrugged. "If this guy wants to babysit the boy in the afternoons, I say let him. The kid can get off the bus here just as easy as getting off at home."

Karen looked undecided. "Well, I ain't driving up here to pick him up."

"You won't have to," Corey said quickly. "I'll walk back. It ain't that far."

Eben expected an argument, but the two *Englischers* just exchanged a glance. "Fine by us, I guess," Wayne said. "But we ain't gonna pay for anything if the kid breaks something or causes a problem."

"Nee," Eben murmured, working to hide his disgust. "I wouldn't hold you responsible."

"Fine, then." Karen shrugged. "Come on, kids. We got to go."

"I'll be here tomorrow afternoon," Corey said as he followed his foster parents to the door.

"Gut. I will see you then," Eben said gruffly.

He locked the door behind them with a vicious twist. He turned, scowling, to find Lilah looking at him, her arms crossed in front of her, eyebrows raised.

"I'd expect you'd be smiling," she told him. "Our plan worked. You got just what you wanted."

Eben sighed. "I guess so." He walked over to collect the broom. Sweeping was Lilah's chore now, but just for today he'd take it back. Maybe it would help him work off a little of his irritation.

"Then why the bad mood?" Lilah called after him.

He paused on his way to the door, his eye catching on Rose's dusty quilting corner. "I don't know," he murmured. "It's just discouraging, the whole of it. Can you believe how those children are being treated? Those people were filling their bellies in a restaurant and letting the two little ones go hungry." He shook his head. "There's too much selfishness and sorrow in this world."

"There is a good bit of that," Lilah agreed, her tone brisk. "But there's a fair bit of good, too, ain't so? Even in this, today."

"I'm having a hard time seeing any good in this right now."

He heard the patter of feet behind him. Lilah scooted ahead of him and stood between him and the door, looking up into his face, her gaze level and calm.

"Well, of course you are. It's hard for you to see the good, Eben, because you're right in the middle of it. You're going to help that boy and his sister. You're going to make a difference in their lives."

"I hope so."

"Oh, you will," she assured him. "You are the good *Gott* has sent to those children, Eben. That's why you can't see the good so well yourself, any more than any of us can see ourselves top to toe. But others see us clear enough, like I see you and the blessings that will be coming to those children because of your help. You just trust in that—and in *Gott*."

Holding his eyes, she nodded firmly. Then she walked briskly away to the storeroom to clean up the children's crumbs.

"I'm a good helper, ain't I, Miss Lilah?" Bethany picked up another jar of jelly and carefully wiped it clean with a soft cloth.

"*Ja*, you are," Lilah assured her with a smile. "I don't know what we'd do without you and your *bruder*."

Corey had been working at Miller's General Store every afternoon for nearly a week now, and in Lilah's opinion, her plan was working out very well. At first, the boy had been nervous and a bit sullen, but when his sulkiness had been met with a kind firmness, he'd soon begun behaving better.

It hadn't hurt that she'd started packing him a substantial after-school snack, which they insisted he eat before starting his daily chores. Food was a great mood improver, she knew.

Yesterday, Corey had brought Bethany along. He'd led her up to the counter by the hand, looking both worried and defiant.

"She ain't gonna get in the way," he'd insisted. "Or bother nobody. I'll take care of her. But can she wait here for me until I'm done?"

Lilah and Eben had exchanged glances, but of course, there'd been no question. Bethany was allowed to stay, and they'd noticed Corey carefully splitting his snack with her. Lilah had guessed Bethany would be back today, so she'd packed another sandwich. And sure enough, here she was.

Today she'd wanted to help, too, so Lilah had found a simple task she could do, and she'd settled in, happy as could be. Why not? Lilah had asked herself. Little girls needed to build good characters, too.

This afternoon, Eben had set Corey to putting together some much needed shelves. Not only were they expecting the new stock from the Fishers, but Eben was planning to go to the big craft fair being held over in Owl Hollow next Saturday. He hoped to find some unusual handmade crafts to freshen up the store's summer stock.

The boy had seemed surprised to be assigned the job of

assembling the shelving and pleased to be trusted with real tools—a hammer and a battery-operated drill. He'd listened attentively to Eben's safety instructions and gotten to work. Now an enthusiastic banging and whirring came from the storeroom at intervals, often startling customers. Eben was keeping an eye on the boy, but mostly was leaving him to work on his own, so Lilah had some private doubts about how well the shelves were being constructed.

But that didn't matter. What mattered was that Corey was working hard and cheerfully, and Eben was whistling as he waited on customers—and made frequent trips to glance casually through the storeroom doorway.

Lilah smiled as she handed Bethany another jar to wipe.

Ja, this plan was working out real well.

Right at closing time, Corey poked his head out of the storeroom.

"I think I'm done," he said uncertainly. "If you wanna come take a look."

"*Ja*, sure," Eben finished totting up something on the legal pad he was scribbling on and started around the counter. Lilah stood up, too.

"Let's go see what your brother's done," she said.

"Okay!" Bethany smiled and trotted happily along beside her.

Eben made it to the storeroom first, and he bent to examine the simple wooden shelves Corey had put together. The boy watched Eben's face nervously, one grubby tennis shoe tapping the floor as he waited on the verdict.

Lilah waited anxiously, too, holding her breath. The shelves looked sturdy enough, but of course, she didn't know much about such things. Eben craned his neck to check on the brackets supporting the shelves and give the structure a good wiggle.

"Gut," he said finally with an approving nod. "You've done real *gut* work here. This'll hold up fine."

"Oh! Uh…all right." Corey tried to hide his relief and pleasure under nonchalance. "Want me to help you carry it out front?"

Eben scratched his beard thoughtfully. "We'll have to figure out where to put it first."

He walked back into the store, and the rest of them followed. Lilah scanned the area, thinking.

"Since the shelving is open backed, it'll have to go against a wall," she said. "Otherwise things will be falling on the floor."

And that was the problem. There wasn't any wall space left open. Well, except for…she kept her eyes carefully away from the little quilting nook. There was plenty of wall space there, and the entire area was being wasted. But of course, she knew without asking that Eben would never agree to change it.

Corey, though, had a puzzled frown on his face. "What about over there?" He nodded toward the little alcove. "You'd have lots of space, 'specially if you moved out that dirty quilt."

Lilah winced, darting a glance at Eben's face. His expression didn't change, but a muscle jumped in his cheek. *"Nee,"* he said quietly. "We'll leave that where it is."

"But why? Nobody even goes over there."

"We can put a backing on the shelves," Eben said. "Then we can stand them up somewhere in the middle of the store. I'll think on it tonight and decide where would be the best spot. Now, we'd best get our last chores done so we can close up and go home."

Corey threw another puzzled look at the quilting corner, but he didn't argue further. He silently picked up the

broom and went out front to sweep off the sidewalk. Eben
had assigned that simple job to him the first day, leaving
Lilah free to work on other end-of-day tasks.

After the children had left, Lilah busied herself with
her work, glancing occasionally at Eben as he tallied up
the day's receipts. He was unusually quiet, and she knew
Corey's remark about changing Rose's quilting area had
bothered him.

She felt a flash of pity, mixed with irritation. It was so
unnecessary, she thought. But she managed to hold her
tongue—or nearly so.

Just as they were finishing, Eben looked up and smiled.
"All done, I think, Lilah. It was a *gut* day. Corey did real
well with that shelving. I was surprised, seeing as how the
boy's had no training. He has the making of a good car-
penter. He'll probably be able to screw the backing on all
by himself, once I cut it to size."

She nodded—and that was when her willpower failed
her. "He's right, you know," she blurted out. "The quilting
area is the best place to put the shelf and the new stock.
You need that space, Eben."

His smile had faded. "I'll find the room elsewhere. The
quilt stays where it is."

"But why? It's doing no good there, not for you and not
for anybody else." She took a few steps forward, her heart
swelling as she tried to think of the right way to say what
she desperately wanted to say. "Not for Rose, either. There
are other ways to remember your wife, Eben. Better ways."

He slammed the ledger he was scribbling in closed.
"What would you know about it?" he muttered bitterly.
"You've never been married."

Lilah blinked. Eben rarely spoke so sharply. She started
to speak, then decided she'd done enough damage. Without

a word, she hurried into the storeroom, collected her lunch cooler and then went out the back door to get her scooter.

She had just wrapped her fingers around the handlebars when the door opened behind her.

"I'm sorry, Lilah. I shouldn't have snapped at you. Please forgive me."

She stood for a moment with her back to him. Then she took a deep breath and turned around.

"You're right," she said. "I've never been married. But that doesn't mean I don't understand what it's like to grieve."

He nodded, and that muscle in his jaw jumped again. "Of course. I know I am not the only one who's suffered sorrow."

"No, you aren't," she agreed bluntly. "There are all kinds of losses in every life, Eben. People are the biggest losses, for sure, but they aren't the only ones. Folks lose lots of other things, too. Dreams. Hopes that just don't come true. We've both of us had our share of sorrows, and we'll have more, mixed with the blessings, like everybody else does. But you can't—" she stopped short.

"Go on," he encouraged her grimly. "Please. Say what you're thinking."

"You probably shouldn't encourage me to do that," she told him dryly. "That's how I get myself in trouble."

"Not this time. Go ahead."

She considered, then shrugged. Fine. If he wanted to hear her thoughts, she'd share them. "You can't keep hanging on to the broken bits and pieces of the past, Eben. Like that quilt there. Rose meant it to be beautiful, but now it's all dusty and starting to fade. It should have been folded away long ago, along with the dreams you two shared. That's a hard thing to do, I know. Maybe I've never had a husband to lose, but I've sure folded up my share of pretty dreams. But when *Gott* has closed the door, hanging on to such things is just…" She struggled for the word. "Unwise," she finished softly.

"Unwise." He echoed the word. "You think I'm acting foolish, Lilah?"

"About most things? *Nee*, I don't. But about this one thing…" She trailed off. "I think maybe you have gotten a little off track."

Silence stretched between them for a few uncomfortable seconds, and Lilah's heart sank. It seemed she'd said too much or the wrong thing or both—as usual. But what was said was said. All she could do now was leave before she made things even worse.

Finally, she turned back to her scooter. "I'd best be getting on home."

"Lilah?"

She didn't turn around. "What?"

"On Monday, I'll set up the new shelf in the quilting corner."

Surprise kept Lilah frozen for a moment. By the time she looked over her shoulder, Eben had already disappeared into the storeroom, and she heard the lock sliding into place.

Chapter Nine

Lilah stood in the summer sunshine, savoring the scent of the Owl Hollow Craft Fair—a mixture of popcorn, funnel cakes and hamburgers. Her stomach rumbled—it was getting on toward noon, and she was hungry.

She didn't mind. Even more than the tempting smells, she savored the feel of Bethany's little fingers entwined with hers as they waited for Eben and Corey to finish examining some leatherwork displayed under a big red tent.

This was turning out to be a real happy day.

The Saturday of the fair dawned clear and not too hot—nice weather for wandering around in a grassy field full of tents and booths showcasing all sorts of handmade crafts. She'd been worried that they'd end up with a soggy day.

The weather hadn't been the only thing she'd been worried about.

On Thursday afternoon, Eben had reminded her that he'd be closing the store on Saturday and going to the fair to scout out new inventory.

"Would you like to come along? I'd like your opinion on the things I consider—if you're not busy that day."

Lilah considered. She'd nothing pressing to do on Saturday, not with the store closed. And Eben really did seem to appreciate her opinion. Their trip to the Fishers' and the new shelf standing against the wall in the quilting area were proof of that.

That was the only change he'd made, so far. Rose's quilt was still gathering dust in its frame. But it was a good start.

"*Ja*, sure," she'd decided. "I'll be happy to come along."

Eben had smiled, the corners of his eyes crinkling in a way that made her stomach go warm. She'd pleased him— and the fact that he'd be so happy to have her along for the day…that pleased her.

Corey and Bethany had been listening to the conversation attentively. They'd said nothing, but the wistfulness on their faces had been obvious.

Eben must have noticed, too, because he'd said, "It's nothing so exciting, this fair. No rides or anything like that. Just a lot of handcrafts for sale that Lilah and I will be looking at for the store."

Two slow, sad nods.

Eben had glanced at Lilah and then back at the children. "But if you would like to come along—"

His invitation had been pounced on before he could finish the sentence. Of course, they'd had to clear the outing with their foster parents, but that had been no trouble. Karen and Wayne Johnson were, as usual, delighted to allow somebody else to watch the children for a day.

So this morning, after Eben had picked her up from Susie's, they'd driven by to collect Corey and Bethany. The children had been very excited at the opportunity to ride in an Amish buggy, and Lilah and Eben had shared several smiles over their enthusiasm.

But Lilah hadn't been so sure their excitement would last. After all, this was a work trip for the adults. She and Eben needed to look at the offerings of every booth, and most of the items for sale wouldn't interest little ones much.

And of course, if something looked promising, Eben would have to talk to the seller about terms, which would slow things down.

It was likely to be a tedious day for the *kinder*. She hadn't been sure how well two *Englisch* children would handle that, and she'd fully expected them to grow impatient.

She'd been wrong.

They'd been at the fair for three hours already, and as near as she could tell, Corey and Bethany had enjoyed every second.

Eben had asked Corey's opinion about some woodwork in one of the first booths, and Corey's awestruck delight at being consulted had been obvious. He'd hovered at Eben's elbow ever since, although like a well-behaved Plain child, he stayed silent until his opinion was asked. Although, Lilah reflected with a smile, it was a *gut* thing that Eben did ask—and frequently. Otherwise, the boy might have exploded. He had ideas about everything.

Fortunately, Bethany seemed perfectly content to walk along with Lilah, holding her hand, looking wide-eyed at the people and the bright displays. Lilah was content, too. It was real pleasant, seeing everything through a little one's eyes—as if the whole world had become fresh and bright again, like it had seemed when she was a child herself.

What a blessing it must be to be a *mamm*, she thought with some sadness.

Eben finished up his discussion with the leatherworker. He and Corey walked back to join them, both of them smiling.

"You look pleased. Your talk must have gone well," Lilah said.

"Ja," Eben said with a nod. "It did. I think the belts will

sell well in the store, and he's giving me a real fair price on them."

"And I'm going to help build a rack to hang 'em on," Corey said happily.

"That's *wunderbaar*," Lilah said approvingly. "That will make them sell all the quicker." She saw Eben's eyes drifting toward the next booth, a display of painted gourds, and she hurried to add, "Maybe now we should take a break. It's near lunchtime, and I'm hungry. I expect the children are, too."

She'd worried Eben might be annoyed at the interruption, but he nodded easily. "*Ja*, you are right. I saw a hamburger stand a few rows over, and they sure smelled good. Will that suit?"

"We don't have any money to buy hamburgers," Bethany said sadly.

"But that's okay," Corey added quickly. "We ain't real hungry anyhow. You can go ahead and eat, though."

Lilah sucked in a short, pained breath, and Eben stiffened, his jaw muscles hardening under his beard. She knew without being told that he was furious. These children had been taught to expect that they'd be allowed to go hungry while adults ate in front of them. She was angry, too, and she opened her mouth to protest.

However, Eben spoke before she could, a gentle kindness in his voice. "Oh, but I am buying lunch for everybody. I invited you all to come, so that is my job to do. Ain't so, Lilah?"

"*Ja*," she managed to say pleasantly. "That is the way it works."

"So, then, will the hamburgers do?" Eben asked. "Or would you rather have something else?"

The children's faces had brightened considerably. "Hamburgers are great!" Corey said.

A few minutes later, they were all settled at a picnic table with hamburgers and french fries in red-and-white-checkered cardboard boxes.

"Before we eat, Lilah and I will pray," Eben explained. "We bow our heads and thank *Gott* silently for our food. You can do the same or not, whichever you like."

"We'll do what you do," Corey said immediately. "But," he added, "if you don't talk when you pray, how will we know when you're done?"

Eben smiled. "My *vadder* used to clear his throat to let the family know the prayer was over. Will that work?"

Corey nodded, looking relieved, and they all bowed their heads together.

Thank you, Gott, *for the blessing of this food*, Lilah prayed earnestly. *And for the joy of spending the day with such sweet children. And thank You for Eben, too. Please forgive me for thinking hard thoughts about him for so many years. He's really a very nice man. Kindhearted and generous and—*

Eben coughed as promised, startling her. Lilah ended her prayer quickly and lifted her head to find Eben looking at her—as if he'd known just what she was praying about.

"Are you all right, Lilah? Your cheeks look a little pink," he said.

"No doubt it's from the sunshine," she said innocently. She took a big bite of her burger before he could ask her any more questions.

The children dug into their lunch happily, and Lilah noticed that they continued imitating the adults. When Lilah put her paper napkin in her lap, Bethany did the same.

When Eben mixed a sprinkle of pepper into his ketchup, Corey copied him.

"Let's pretend we're a family," Bethany said suddenly.

Eben and Lilah exchanged surprised glances. Corey looked embarrassed and shook his head.

"Don't be silly. They ain't gonna want to do that," Corey said. "You're messing everything up, Bethany. Hush and eat your food."

"She's not messing anything up," Eben said. "I know what she means. It does feel like we're a family today."

Lilah's heart jumped. Suddenly, she didn't know where to look, and she took another bite of her hamburger to cover her confusion.

Bethany nodded. "Yes! Lilah's the mommy, and you're the daddy, and we're your kids." When her brother frowned at her, she added defensively, "It's only pretend, Corey. Just for today."

"It's a nice game to play," Eben agreed gently. "And since I am the *daed* today, I tell you what—I am going to give you each ten dollars to spend here at the fair."

"Really?" Corey's eyes were wide—and slightly skeptical. "You're gonna give us money?"

"*Ja*. You both deserve a treat for helping so much at the store. You can buy whatever you like to take home."

As the children chattered excitedly about what they thought they would buy, Lilah took a sip of her sweet tea. Suddenly, she couldn't eat another bite. The burger was very good, but there was no way she could get it past the lump that had formed in her throat.

And that, she told herself, was very silly. The day was going so nicely. The children were enjoying themselves, and Eben was finding some good items for the store. She couldn't have hoped for a better day. There was no reason she should feel as if she wanted to cry, just because a little girl wanted to pretend Lilah was her *mamm*.

When she could speak, she murmured in *Deutsch*, "That was a very generous thing to do, giving them money to spend."

Eben shrugged, looking embarrassed. "What I said was true. They have both worked and tried hard to be helpful. Besides, having a little money to spend teaches wisdom. If they spend wisely, they will be happy. If they spend foolishly, they will learn to think more carefully about their purchases. Either way, it is a *gut* thing."

Lilah glanced at the children's rapidly disappearing lunches. "They may end up buying something else to eat." She'd suspected the children wouldn't have had a very good breakfast, so she'd brought along a little bag of Susie's oatmeal raisin cookies. They'd eaten every single one, but cookies didn't have much staying power with growing children, especially not when they'd spent the morning walking around in the fresh air.

"Nee," Eben shook his head. "They'll not buy food with their spending money. If they want another hamburger, I will buy it for them." He glanced toward the food stand and then turned away quickly. *"Ach,"* he muttered under his breath.

Lilah frowned. "What's wrong?"

He shot her an embarrassed look. "Mary Glick is over there."

Sure enough, the older woman, a member of their church, stood at the burger booth, placing an order. Another gray-haired woman was with her, someone Lilah didn't recognize.

She frowned, puzzled at Eben's obvious distress.

"So? Lots of Plain folks came to the fair today." There'd

been a long row of horses and buggies under the shade trees where they'd left Blaze. "Why does it matter to you if she's here?"

Eben glanced at Corey and Bethany. The children were busy eating the last of their burgers, talking between bites. He lowered his voice and continued speaking in *Deutsch*.

"Mary…she's a very nice woman, but I try to avoid her when I can."

Lilah was now thoroughly confused. "But why?"

"Because she always…" Eben looked as if he'd just sat down on a nail. "It's hard to explain."

"Eben?" Just at that moment, Mary called to them, waving. "Hello! I thought that was you."

Leaving her friend at the stand, Mary walked over to their table. She scanned their group, her brown eyes thoughtful behind her round spectacles. "Hello, Lilah." One brow lifted. "You two are here together?"

Eben seemed to be struggling for an answer, so Lilah smiled. "*Ja*. We came here to look at new items for the store. And we brought some friends with us." She nodded at the children. "This is Bethany, and that's Corey."

"Ah! These must be the children who've been helping you in your store. I've heard about that from several folks. It's very nice to finally meet you."

Like Eben, the *kinder* seemed to be struck silent. They stared back at the stranger, their eyes wide. Ketchup was smeared on Bethany's chin. Lilah leaned close to wipe it off, whispering, "You should say it is good to meet her, too."

"It's good to meet her, too," Bethany parroted obediently.

Mary laughed. "What a *gut* girl," she said. Then she turned her attention back to Eben. "So? Have you found many nice things for your store?"

"A good many, *ja*," Eben replied.

"How exciting. I will have to come see. And, of course, I will bring my Anna. I am sure she will want to see, too. The outing will do her good. She doesn't get out so much, now that Henry is gone. But she enjoys visiting your store, and you two haven't had much chance to talk lately."

Lilah's eyes narrowed. Suddenly, it all made sense—both Mary's eager friendliness and Eben's desperate desire to avoid her.

Twenty-three-year-old Anna Speicher was Mary's daughter. Almost two years ago, when Anna was expecting their first child, her husband, Henry, had been killed in a farming accident. Mary was obviously set on Eben as a potential new son-in-law, and she was being none too subtle about it. If Eben wasn't interested, no wonder he was avoiding her. At the moment, his face was beet red, and he didn't seem to know what to say.

But she did.

"Bring Anna by anytime," Lilah said brightly. "Eben is usually too busy to talk, but I'm at the store every day now. I can show you whatever you'd like to see, and of course, I would love to visit with you and Anna both."

"Oh!" Mary seemed taken aback. "*Denki*, Lilah. That would be…kind." Her companion walked up, balancing two burgers in her hands. Mary introduced her quickly as her *kossin* Bertha, visiting from Ohio. Then she excused herself so that they could go have their lunches.

Lilah waved goodbye to them with a cheerful smile. She looked over to find Eben studying her. His embarrassment had vanished, and his lips were twitching, as if he were amused.

But all he said was, "Does anybody want more to eat? I'm happy to buy another hamburger if anyone's still hungry."

Although the children had eaten every scrap of their

lunches, they shook their heads. Lilah wasn't sure if they were shy about accepting more food or if they were just eager to start shopping.

No matter. She'd buy a funnel cake for them to eat on the way home, Lilah decided, and let them get about their fun.

Corey and Eben were deep in a conversation about the belt rack they were planning to build, so Lilah began gathering up their trash. She smiled as Bethany helped, carefully wadding up the paper napkins and tucking them inside the empty checkerboard boxes.

"We'll take this to the trash can together," Lilah suggested. "And then maybe we visit the restroom, *ja*?" The children had each downed a jumbo-size drink, so she figured that was a smart move. She threw a look at Eben and nodded toward Corey.

Understanding dawned in Eben's eyes. "We'll do the same," he decided.

Bethany and Lilah's path brought them near to Mary and Bertha's table. Lilah was prepared to speak, but Mary was too busy talking to notice them.

"Such a shame," the older woman was saying sadly in *Deutsch*. "Not about my Anna so much. She's always been real well-liked, and she's sure to make a good second marriage sooner or later. It's Eben I feel sorry for. He can't seem to get past his grief over losing Rose, but it's plain the man's lonesome. Why else would he have taken two little *Englisch* children under his wing?"

Bertha said, dipping a fry into some ketchup, "It's kind of him."

"*Ja*, but sad, too. Eben's always been softhearted about children, and folks who've seen them at the store say he's acting as if they were his own son and daughter." She clucked her tongue. "But, of course, they're *Englischers*, so that can never work out. I don't know what the poor man's thinking. His heart's going to get broken again, you wait and see."

"What about that woman he's with? She seems nice enough. Do you think maybe..." Mary shook her head.

"Eben and Lilah? Not likely. She's never been the sort that men pay attention to. She works at his store, that's all. Besides, Eben's had enough disappointments in his life already. He'd be much happier with a wife like my Anna. He'd be a fine stepfather for our little Matthew, and he and Anna could have a nice, big family of their own, too. Lilah's forty if she's a day, and—"

"Shhh." Bertha warned. She'd finally caught sight of Lilah and Bethany, now on their way back from the trash can. Mary cleared her throat and began talking loudly about her garden.

As Lilah passed their table, she kept her eyes down. She did her best to look as if she hadn't heard, as if she was only listening to Bethany's chatter about a stuffed owl she'd seen and might want for her treat.

But, of course, she had heard. And although she was trying her best not to care, Mary's words had brushed the bloom right off her happy day.

Not so much because of what Mary had said about her. That had stung, but Lilah knew it was only what most people thought and were too kind to say out loud.

But what she'd said about Eben? That did trouble her— because Mary was right. Eben might not have been blessed with children of his own, but he had a father's heart, just the same, a heart that couldn't help but care deeply about Corey and Bethany.

And there was no doubt the children needed such care, but they were, as Mary had pointed out, *Englischers*. And as if that weren't problem enough, they were also foster children, which meant that their home wasn't a permanent one.

Sooner or later, the children would likely be moved to a different family, and who knew if she and Eben would ever see them again?

And when that happened, just as Mary had said—and thanks to Lilah's bright idea—Eben's *gut*, kind heart would be broken.

Again.

Several hours later, Eben flicked the reins on Blaze's back, and he and Lilah pulled out of the Johnsons' driveway to start the last lap of their day's journey.

He hadn't liked leaving the children there. They'd been so happy right up to the last, their faces sprinkled with powdered sugar from the funnel cake Lilah had given them. But the minute the buggy had rolled into the Johnsons' yard, their smiles had faded.

But he'd had no choice in the matter, he told himself, and what couldn't be helped had to be endured. Better to thank *Gott* for the blessings of the day.

And there had been plenty of those.

Not only had he found lots of new stock for the store, but he'd had a real nice time. The children had, too. After careful deliberation, Bethany had decided on a toy owl as her treat. It had cost a little more than the ten dollars he'd offered, but Eben had intended to make up the small difference.

Or he would have done, if he'd had the chance. Before he could offer, Corey had made up the difference from his own money. When Eben attempted to intervene, Corey had shaken his head.

"You're being nice, but you ain't really our daddy. She's my sister, and it's my job to look after her."

Eben hadn't felt right about pushing it, so he'd stayed quiet—and bought the children some candies to take home with them.

Now he just had to take Lilah back to Susie's, and he could go home himself.

Pleasant though the day had been, it had also been long, and he was tired. He should be happy to get himself home, see to his chores and go to bed. Lilah was probably tired, too. She'd been very quiet on the ride home, and for Lilah that was unusual.

So he should have kept Blaze going at a brisk pace and brought this day to its end. Instead, he tugged gently on the reins, slowing the gelding down a little. No point hurrying too much. He cleared his throat.

"I think the little ones had a happy time today," he said. "Although, it troubled me a bit, what Corey said about it being his job to look after his sister."

Lilah kept her eyes on the road. "I suppose it is his job, whether we like it or not."

Eben glanced at her, surprised. "He's only a boy, barely able to look after himself. Taking care of Bethany should be the job of those foster parents."

Lilah sighed and dropped her gaze to her hands, folded in her lap. "Maybe it should be. But even if the Johnsons were better people, what Corey said would still be true. Foster care isn't meant to last forever. Children get moved from home to home all the time. Bethany and Corey will have to depend on each other."

Eben's frown deepened. He didn't know much about this foster care business, but that seemed wrong to him. "You mean they often change parents, these children?"

"They do, from what I understand. Children can get moved for lots of different reasons."

"So Corey and Bethany could be moved someplace new, then." He thought this over. While he hoped if the little ones did get moved, it would be to a much better place, he realized that such a thing would likely put an end to their time at the store—and to little outings like this one.

That was a shame. He'd really enjoyed today—more than he'd enjoyed anything in a very long time. Bethany hadn't been the only one pretending they were a family— he'd almost felt like a *daed*, showing the children around the fair, buying them little treats.

And Lilah—he'd enjoyed spending time with her, too. She was fun to be with, smiling, laughing and never complaining. But she was honest, too, like when she'd told him it was time for lunch. He'd not had to guess about it—she'd just told him it was time to stop and eat.

He liked that. A man could feel restful in the company of such a woman, knowing she'd speak right up if there was something wrong.

She'd spoken up about something else, too, he remembered.

"I want to thank you," he said. "For what you said back there to Mary Glick. I appreciated it. She's been trying to match me up with her Anna, and to be honest, I'm running out of polite ways to sidestep her."

Lilah had been gazing out the side of the buggy at the passing scenery. She shifted to look at him, her face shadowed underneath her black bonnet. "I don't know. Maybe I shouldn't have said anything."

He frowned. "What do you mean?"

"Maybe you shouldn't be sidestepping Mary's matchmaking at all."

"Vass?"

She shrugged, turning her eyes toward the road ahead.

"Well, Anna's a nice, sweet woman, ain't so? Don't you think she'd make any man a fine wife?"

He couldn't quite believe what he was hearing. "Any man but me, sure. I'm not interested. And I never pegged you as a matchmaker, Lilah."

"I'm not, usually. But in this case…"

"This case is no different from all the others," he assured her irritably. "I've had more than enough of this kind of thing over the past few years. Every time I turn around, it seems like another woman's trying to convince me to marry her. And if it's not the woman herself, it's her *mamm*."

"You can hardly blame them."

He blinked. "I'm surprised to hear you say that."

She turned back toward him. "Why? Because I said I didn't like you so much? That doesn't mean you wouldn't suit another woman. And anyhow—" she shrugged "—now that I've got to know you better, it turns out you're not so bad, after all."

Eben chuckled. Lilah was always saying something unexpected. "That's *gut* to know, but it's not what I meant." He wasn't sure how best to explain. "I'd just not expect you to be nagging at me—or anybody else—to get married. You've always seemed real happy to be single."

"Happy?" The disbelief in her voice was obvious. "Me? Not to be married?"

"Well, *ja*. At least, you've always seemed so. I mean, sure, some women couldn't handle being alone, but you… you always seemed real strong-minded. Not the kind of person who needed a husband to be content with her life. Not that it's a bad thing," he hurried to add. "In fact, it's one of the reasons I hired you to work at the store. Like I said, Mary Glick's not the only one who thinks I should be marrying again. There've been plenty of others, too, and one or two of the women I hired were among them. But I knew with you, I'd not have to worry about any of that nonsense."

"Nonsense." She stared at him, her expression unreadable. "You think it's nonsense for a woman to want a home and a family of her own?"

Eben felt as if he'd stepped unexpectedly off into some very deep water—and forgotten how to swim. "Well, not for most women. But like I said, you've chosen differently, and—"

That was as far as he got.

"I didn't get to choose, Eben. That's the difference. No man ever asked me to marry him."

He was thankful for the dimming light because he could only imagine how red his face was. He fumbled for something to say—anything that might turn this awful conversation around. "Well, even so, you wouldn't have wanted to marry me, so—"

"If you don't slow down, you're going to miss Susie's house," she interrupted.

He reined in Blaze quickly, turning the buggy sharply into the driveway. He tried to think of something to say to smooth things over, but before he could, Lilah had jumped out of the buggy.

"It's getting dark," she said over her shoulder. "Best be careful driving home."

"I will. *Mach's gut*, Lilah," he called after her. The only response he got was an irritated wave.

He mulled their conversation over as he drove Blaze home and did his evening chores. He was still thinking about it when he walked into his house and hung his hat on the peg by the door.

The kitchen was empty and dark. It always was, but somehow after a day spent in bright sunshine and happy company, it felt worse than usual. He was hit with a sudden, sharp pang of loneliness, and something Susie had once said stirred in his memory.

You're not the only person in the world with troubles.

Nee, of course he wasn't. Other folks were lonely, too. Like Anna, who'd lost her husband so young and was now left to raise her little son alone. And Lilah, who'd never had a husband to begin with.

The bishop had said more than once that it was a man's duty to marry—a duty to the church and to the community, both. Honestly, Eben hadn't paid a lot of attention to those hints since Rose's death.

He'd never thought that by choosing not to remarry, he was somehow cheating a woman out of a home and a family. A woman like Anna Speicher.

Or Lilah.

It was something to think on, he decided. But not tonight. Tomorrow, maybe. When his wits were fresher.

But as he finished his nighttime routine, his thoughts kept drifting back to the idea of marriage. And for the first time in many years, Rose's face wasn't the first that came to his mind.

Neither was Anna Speicher's.

Chapter Ten

Early the following Wednesday morning, Lilah quickly cleared away the mess from putting together the day's lunches for herself, Eben and the children. As she wiped crumbs off the counter, she doubtfully eyed the tall stack of roast beef sandwiches she'd just made.

"I'm not sure these are all going to fit in the cooler."

"It'll be a near thing if they do," Susie observed from her seat at the kitchen table. "The lunches you're taking to the store get bigger every day." She took another sip of her coffee. "You keep feeding all those folks, you're going to need a larger cooler."

"I can't fit a bigger one in my scooter basket. But *ja*, it's getting to be a problem. Corey and Bethany receive free school lunches, but they're still so hungry when they get to the store that they can polish off two sandwiches each." A troublesome idea occurred to her. "Is it a problem, me taking so much food from the kitchen every day? I should have thought of that—it's an extra expense. I should be paying you for it."

"*Nee*, don't you worry about that." Susie flapped a careless hand. "The day I can't send food out of my kitchen to feed hungry children is the day I hang up my apron." She raised her cup back to her mouth, but before she took a sip, she murmured, "Of course, the children aren't the only ones you're feeding, ain't so? How's Eben liking the lunches?"

Lilah kept her gaze down as she finished layering the sandwiches in the cooler. "He seems to appreciate them." She closed the lid with some difficulty.

She didn't want to talk about Eben. Since their conversation in the buggy last Saturday, things had been different between the two of them. Uncomfortable. After their newfound friendship, this change felt like putting on a pair of stiff shoes after running barefoot all summer. She had nobody to blame but herself, though. It was her fault he acted so awkward and strange around her now.

She'd been too outspoken, as usual. She shouldn't have shared how she felt about being unmarried. No doubt she'd come across as a bitter and unhappy woman, and she wasn't, truly.

Well, most of the time, she wasn't.

But after spending the day with Eben and the children, she'd had a sweet taste of what it might have felt like to have a family of her own. And she'd known that Eben had felt the same. Not about her, obviously. He'd made that clear. But about the children, for sure.

And that troubled her.

Working with Eben, she'd gotten to know him a lot better, and little by little, her opinion of him had shifted. Maybe sometimes he spoke without thinking, but she could hardly fault him for that.

He was a very kind man, a strong, sensible man, but he had a real soft heart, Eben did, and such hearts were easily broken. Just look at how long he'd grieved over Rose. Most widowers in the community remarried after a year or so, with full approval of the church.

But not Eben.

And most men she knew, even the kindhearted ones, wouldn't have taken such trouble over two neglected little *Englischers*.

But Eben had.

If he had a family, a wife or children of his own, there'd be nothing to worry over. That was why she'd brought up Anna Speicher—because Mary was right. If Eben married someone like Anna, if he had little Matthew and later children of his own to love, then his heart wouldn't break when Corey and Bethany moved on.

Because Eben didn't only need a wife. He needed a family, too, a nice, big family like Mark Fisher had. Anybody could see that.

Well, almost anybody.

Susie was chuckling as she carried her breakfast dishes to the sink. "Taking him those lunches was a *schmaert* idea. I notice that Eben sure seems interested in spending extra time with you these days, taking you out to the Fishers and to craft fairs and such." She rinsed her coffee cup out. "That's a big step for him. But then, my *grossmammi* always said that good food was the surest way to any man's heart."

Lilah had gathered up her things and was on her way to the door, but she stopped midway, banging the cooler down on the kitchen table so hard that Susie's eyes widened.

"I'm not taking him the lunches so he'll like me. I pack him food for the same reason I pack it for the *kinder*. Because we have extra, and I feel sorry for him."

"Is that so?" Susie considered her with lifted brows— and a twinkle in her eye. "Are you sure Eben knows that?"

"Of course he does. If he thought any different he would never have accepted the lunches in the first place. And that's another thing," Lilah went on hotly, "I really wish that you would stop trying to match me and Eben up, Susie. It's a waste of time. He's made it very clear he's not interested. And I'm not—" She'd started to say *I'm not interested in him, either*. But for some reason, the words stuck in her throat.

"Not interested?" Susie's smile faded. "When you say he made it clear—"

"Very clear," Lilah corrected stubbornly.

"You're not talking about all those years ago, back when he had his heart set on Rose? Because things change, and—"

"*Nee*, not then. He said so Saturday, on the ride home from Owl Hollow. In fact, in his opinion, I am a woman who was meant to be single."

Those words—coming so soon after their happy day together—had hit a sore spot. But, of course, Eben and Mary Glick were right. For some reason, even back when she was young and her friends were getting married left and right, Lilah had never been the sort boys looked at with stars in their eyes.

She knew that. She'd even come to accept it. But it was still not very pleasant to have it pointed out twice in one day.

"Eben said you were meant to be single?" Susie's brows drew together into a frown. "What an unkind thing to say!"

"He wasn't being unkind." Not on purpose anyhow. "He was being honest and just saying what everybody else has thought for years. He said it's why he hired me to work at his store. Because he's tired of people trying to marry him off, and he knew there'd be no worries about that sort of nonsense with me."

"Nonsense." Susie stood by the sink, the clean cup forgotten in her hand. For once in her life, she seemed at a loss for words. "Is that what he said? Maybe he didn't mean to be unkind, but he was certainly being very thoughtless."

Somehow Susie's indignation made Lilah feel worse. "It was partly my fault. I'm the one who brought up the subject of marriage. As usual, I let my tongue run away with me, and I…said something I shouldn't have."

"Oh, Lilah!" Susie's sympathetic moan made no sense for a second. Then Lilah understood. Susie, whose mind was never far from matchmaking, thought she'd confessed romantic feelings for Eben—and been turned down. Lilah hurried to explain.

"It was nothing like that, Susie! I've better sense."

"Oh!" Susie blinked. "Well, *gut*. Then whatever you said, he deserved it." Her friend paused. "If you don't mind me asking, what exactly did you say?"

"I just…suggested he should take notice of Anna Speicher."

"*Vass?* But why on earth would you say such a thing to him?" Susie seemed almost comically horrified.

"Because it's true. Eben's the sort who needs a wife and a family, and Anna's a very sweet girl and her little boy needs a father, and—" For some reason, the words were getting more and more difficult to say, and Lilah found herself growing irritated. "In any case, you can hardly fuss at me—or anybody else—for trying a little matchmaking, Susie Raber!"

"Maybe not." Susie was watching her closely now, a funny glint in her eye. "But it doesn't sound like Eben took kindly to the suggestion."

"*Nee*, he didn't, and now he's acting all bashful and strange around me."

"Is he now?" Susie looked thoughtful. "Bashful and

strange. Eben Miller? That must have been quite a buggy ride."

"I wish I'd kept quiet because it's uncomfortable working at the store together now. But since I need the income, there's not much I can do."

"Isn't there?" Susie murmured. When Lilah shot her a questioning look, she sighed. "I have something to confess, and I'm afraid you're going to be very angry with me. Wait here a second."

Susie set down her cup and walked into the living room. She rummaged in a drawer for a second, then returned with a business card. She held it out silently.

Lilah took the card and studied it, puzzled. "Plain Goods? What's that?"

"A store, a big one, over in Milton. Their Amish community there is turning more to tourism to make ends meet, and this store is a huge attraction. From what I've heard, they can't keep things in stock. Especially not quilts."

"Quilts?" Lilah looked back down at the card. "Do you think they'd be interested in mine?"

"I'm sure of it. Their owner came into the bakery a few weeks ago, and he saw that quilt you made hanging on the wall. He gave me this card and told me if you were interested in selling any on consignment to let him know. But I didn't tell you about it, and I'm very sorry, Lilah. I hope you can forgive me."

"Of course. But why, Susie? Why wouldn't you tell me such a thing?"

Susie clasped her hands together in front of her apron. "It was back when you were just getting settled at Eben's store. I thought maybe it wasn't the best timing. But now..." She shrugged. "Who knows? Maybe the timing is just right."

Lilah wasn't sure what Susie meant, but at the moment,

she didn't care. This was very good news. Somebody finally wanted to buy her quilts. A big store in a busy community that was courting tourism.

This was a fine opportunity. She needed to think it over thoroughly, though, because what Mary and Eben had said might have been hard to hear, but it was also true. She was likely to be alone all her life, and if she didn't want to be a burden to her brothers, she'd need to manage her business wisely.

She turned the situation over in her mind all the way to the store, and her thoughts drifted back to it throughout the morning. Eben looked at her funny a few times, especially when he had to ask her twice to help a customer find some spices.

By lunchtime, she'd come to a decision. As soon as he flipped the sign over, she spoke up.

"If it's all right, I think I will work through lunch today. I can go ahead and refill the shelves, and I'd like to leave an hour early. I have an important phone call to make."

Eben nodded slowly, his brow furrowed. "*Ja*, of course." He shifted his weight from one boot to the other. "You can leave early if you want. But why not just use the store phone? You're welcome to that, if it would be easier."

She'd considered that, but she hadn't liked to ask the favor. Still, it would be more convenient than walking to the nearest phone shack, for sure.

"I don't mean to be nosy, but is everything all right?" Eben was asking. "I hope your family's all doing well."

"Oh, they are. It's nothing like that."

"I'm glad to hear it. And, as I said, you're welcome to use the phone here." He shifted his feet again and cleared his throat. "In fact, maybe that could free up your afternoon a little. Mark Fisher sent word that our new order was ready to pick up. I was thinking of driving out there after clos-ing today. We could both go and take Corey and Bethany with us. It might be fun for them playing with the Fisher children, seeing the animals and all. Don't you think?"

Ja, they would like that, very much. And honestly, so would she. But...

Riding in a buggy with Eben, while two children chat-tered in the back, pretending they were a family. As won-derful as that sounded, she didn't think it was a wise idea.

Because the truth was, they weren't a family, and they never could be.

Eben's hopes for a pleasant afternoon sank when Lilah shook her head.

"I don't think I can spare the time. This phone call I have to make—it's to a store owner over in Milton. The fellow who owns Plain Goods. Have you heard of him?"

"*Ja*, I have. I went to his store once, to see what it was like." He'd gone out of curiosity. The place was four times the size of his and did a lot more business, and he'd hoped to learn some things he could apply here in Hickory Springs.

"Do you think the owner is someone who'd be fair in his dealings?"

"I don't know him well enough to say." He paused, a sense of dread growing in his heart. "Lilah, are you look-ing for another job?"

He'd worried something like this might happen. Ever since that buggy ride, he'd felt unsettled around her, and near as he could tell, she felt just as strange around him.

Not that he knew much about how women felt about things—obviously.

He'd meant to pay her a compliment, pointing out her independence and her strength. He admired those qualities, very much, but plainly she'd not taken his words the way he'd intended.

And that wasn't the worst of it. Finding out that Lilah would've liked to have been married—mixed with spending time with her, Corey and Bethany—had put some surprising ideas in his head.

Bethany wasn't the only one doing some pretending these days. Every time he looked at Lilah now, he found himself imagining what it would be like to have her as his wife, to have her company not only at the store, but also in his home every evening.

Such thoughts, pleasant as they were, had done him no favors. Lately, every time he looked in Lilah's direction— which he did far too often—he felt like a silly schoolboy. Acted like one, too, stumbling over both his feet and his words.

He'd made a fool of himself more than once over the past few days, and he'd noticed Lilah looking at him funny a few times. Now she was thinking of quitting and moving to Milton?

He didn't like the idea of that at all.

To his relief, Lilah shook her head. "Not exactly. I mean, I'm not looking to work for him, but I'm thinking of doing some business with him. He's interested in my quilts."

"Your quilts?"

"Yes." He listened as she recounted a conversation she'd had with Susie. "I've been thinking it over. Of course, I've got several he can have right away, if he gives me good terms on them. But if he sells them as fast as Susie seems to think he will, I'll need to make more, and I've little time for sewing these days. So I won't have time to spare after work anymore. I may even have to cut back on my working hours."

He was liking this less and less. But what could he do about it? Nothing. Unless…he glanced over toward Rose's old quilting nook, dusty and quiet. He'd added the new shelf as he'd told Lilah he would, but that was the only change he'd made. And he'd politely turned down her eager offer to give the whole area a good scrubbing.

Lilah was still talking about the potential deal with the other store, but Eben was barely listening. Instead, he was trying his best to think this through before he spoke.

He wasn't sure it was the right thing to do, and he felt a little guilty about it. But it might very well mend the fences between them and stop Lilah from spending less time in the store in one move.

"I'll sell your quilts here."

He blurted the words out, interrupting her in mid-sentence. She stopped, her mouth and eyes both round with astonishment.

"But, you said—"

"I know what I said. I've changed my mind." He hoped desperately that she wouldn't ask him any more than that.

But this was Lilah. So, of course, she did.

"Why?"

Because I don't want you to leave. Because I'd like to spend more time with you, not less. Because…

He couldn't say those things. So he just said, "I've already started using part of that space for the new stock I'm getting in from the Fishers. I might as well use it all. And if quilts are selling that well in Milton, they're likely to sell well here, too."

"Probably so." She nodded slowly, but he thought she looked a little disappointed. "That all makes sense, I suppose."

He swallowed. "And Rose has been gone for three years. I think it's...time to make some changes."

Her face changed into a soft sympathy. *"Ja,"* she said. "I think so, too." And then because she was Lilah, she added, "Past time."

"I'll take the quilt off the frame," he said. He wasn't looking forward to that. He'd helped Rose put that quilt in the frame all those years ago. And he'd known even then, deep in his heart, that she'd probably not live to finish it.

But Rose had hoped otherwise. She'd been so determined—

"I can help you," Lilah offered gently. "Take it out and put it away, I mean. It needs cleaning, and that could be difficult, being as it's unfinished. But—"

"Denki, but no, I can handle it. I've got this trip out to the Fishers to tend to first. But after that. Then you can put your own quilts for sale in there, however you like."

Lilah looked uncertain. "I don't mean to seem ungrateful. I know this is difficult for you. But as you pointed out, I've no husband to provide for me and never will. So I have to think about my finances carefully. What terms will you offer for the quilts?"

"Terms?" He'd not thought of that at all, and her reminder about that disastrous conversation made him flinch guiltily. "I've no terms. You're welcome to sell them here and keep whatever money you make."

Her eyes widened. "That hardly seems fair to you! I'll be taking up a good bit of your store space. You should get a percentage."

"As long as you work here, you can use the space for nothing. Consider it repayment for the extra help you've given me, what with the craft fair and picking things out at the Fishers. I'll probably need more of that now and then, so we can consider the space for your quilts the return of the favor."

"Oh." She looked uncertain. "I don't know. Like I said, I'll need my free time for sewing."

"It'll only be now and again. Besides, think of the time you'll save, not having to run back and forth to Milton carrying quilts."

She still didn't look convinced, but she nodded. "I suppose you're right. This seems a very fair offer. For me, anyway. I'm not so sure you're getting a good bargain."

"I'll worry about that. Now, let's eat lunch so we can reopen the store on time."

"All right." She still seemed stunned, but she headed for the storeroom. "I brought roast beef sandwiches today," she called over her shoulder.

"Those are my favorite," he said. "So, see? I'm not getting such a poor bargain after all."

He was rewarded by a soft laugh, and a minute later, she handed him a thick sandwich with a tentative smile.

"Do you want to eat out back again? It's nice weather today, and the butterflies are everywhere, enjoying the flowers."

He did want to, very badly. And the strength of that longing he felt to sit outside in the sunshine and enjoy a few precious moments alone with Lilah—that was part of the reason he shook his head.

"I think I'll eat inside today, by myself. Just for this one last time," he said.

Lilah's face softened. "I understand," she said. Then she slipped away, leaving him alone.

Eben carried his lunch over to the quilting corner and sat down, just as he had so many times before. He studied the dusty quilt stretched over the frame, lingering on each square in its turn and reminding himself of what it meant.

That was Rose's life, those squares. She'd given that short life to him, and he'd not forget it—he'd not forget her. He'd no idea what would come next for him, whether these surprising, new hopes would ever come to anything at all.

It seemed a little unlikely.

But even if *Gott* did bless him with new happiness, he'd never forget the old.

He was unusually quiet that afternoon, and he noticed Lilah shooting thoughtful glances his way.

He wasn't being very good company, he knew. Maybe that was why, later, when he and the excited children were getting ready for the ride over to the Fishers, she said she'd decided not to come along, after all.

"I'm a little tired today, and I need to sort my quilts and get them ready for sale. I can close up here so that you all can go ahead. I know how to do it, and that way you can leave earlier. But," she added quickly, "I'll go the next time when there are new items to look at. All right?"

Eben was deeply disappointed, and he wanted to argue. On the other hand, he also didn't want to risk saying the wrong thing.

So he nodded. "Next time, then."

But by the time he was halfway to the Fishers, he wished he'd insisted Lilah come along.

At least the children were enjoying themselves. At first, they'd been disappointed that Lilah wasn't with them, but now they chattered like happy squirrels in the back of the buggy. He liked the sound of that. He did.

But the seat beside him felt mighty empty.

Maybe it wouldn't be so empty next time, he reminded

himself. She'd agreed to come along on the next trip. He'd make sure there was one—and soon.

Ja, it had been a good idea, offering to let her have the space for her quilts, he decided as the buggy rolled placidly through the quiet summer afternoon. It had put a stop to her idea of talking to the fellow at Plain Goods, for one thing.

He was thankful for that. And he didn't have to feel guilty about it because she'd never have gotten such a *gut* deal from that other store.

By the time they'd reached the Fisher farm, his spirits had lifted. And seeing Corey and Bethany quickly welcomed into the herd of children made him smile.

Ruth was on the front porch with one of the older girls, unpinning clean laundry from a clothesline. She left her daughter to the task and hurried down the steps to speak to Eben.

"Lilah didn't come today? I'm sorry. I was looking forward to seeing her."

"She stayed behind to close up the store. But she's looking forward to coming next time."

Ruth smiled and nodded at the two *Englisch* children, currently balancing on the bottom rung of a wooden fence. They were inspecting a brand-new calf and looked delighted. "I see you did bring some helpers with you, though. Are those the two foster children who've been helping you at the store?"

"Ja." There was no point asking her how she knew about that. Word traveled fast in a small Plain community, particularly among the women. "Their names are Corey and Bethany Bender. I hope it's all right that I brought them along."

"Of course! Mark and I are very happy to have them

visit." She smiled at him, leaned a bit closer and lowered her voice. "We are very happy for you, too, Eben."

With that, she turned and headed briskly back to the porch. Eben thought over her remark as he went over the new order with Mark. When everything had been checked, he closed the carton and shot his friend a glance.

"Can I ask you a question?"

"*Ja*, sure."

"Ruth just told me you two were happy for me. What did she mean by that?"

"*Ach.*" Mark shrugged, looking uncomfortable. "You know how the women are, Eben."

"I'm out of practice figuring them out, it seems. Maybe you'd better explain."

Mark hesitated. "She meant nothing by it except that we're all glad to see you taking notice again. That's all."

"Taking notice. You're talking about Lilah?"

"I'm talking about nothing. And neither should she be. It's your own business, at least for now. Well. Yours and Lilah's. Now, let's get these boxes out to your buggy."

Mark hefted a box up and went through the open doorway. Eben should have followed, but instead he stood where he was, staring.

And thinking, hard.

So, that was what people were saying. That he was taking notice again—of Lilah.

And maybe he was.

He was still getting used to the idea himself, and he certain sure hadn't said anything to Lilah—and he'd not planned on it, either. Not yet. He was still adjusting to the idea of taking down Rose's quilt.

But now he might not have much of a choice. Once folks saw her quilts displayed in Rose's old corner... Then the gossip would heat up, for certain sure. It would be like striking a match to a pile of autumn leaves.

And he'd no idea how Lilah would react to that.

Ja. He was in trouble.

Chapter Eleven

After Eben and the children had left, Lilah studied the quilt corner, her heart pounding with excitement.

This could work well.

There was plenty of space to display the quilts she already had made. She could arrange a few on the walls and others on racks. She'd noticed two or three quilting racks in the back of the storeroom. A little dusting and polishing, and they'd be perfect.

She could make some smaller pieces, too. Some pot holders, possibly, each one made from a different quilt square. She had a feeling that Eben's customers would like those, and since they were less expensive, they'd likely move quickly. She could make some wall hangings and baby quilts, too.

There were all kinds of possibilities. And because of Eben's kind offer to allow her to sell her quilts here for free, she'd make a fine profit, too. She wondered if maybe this generosity was his way of making up for his thoughtless comment in the buggy.

Maybe. But maybe not. Eben was kind to everyone, always, and he was generous to a fault. Her gaze dropped to Rose's unfinished quilt, and her conscience poked her.

Ja, Eben was being very unselfish, but she certainly

wasn't. Look at her, standing here being so excited over her own happy prospects, not thinking about anybody else but herself.

She knew better. She'd been taught from birth that selfishness was sinful. It was wrong to think only of herself. Wrong not to consider the feelings and the pain of other people.

This would be a very hard thing for Eben, taking down his late wife's quilt. A good thing, in Lilah's opinion. A healthy thing.

But still, not easy.

She studied the quilt, tracing a square featuring an appliquéd apple tree, noting the neat, even stitching. A shame this quilt had not been completed. It would have been a pretty one and a sweet reminder of Rose. Instead it was dirty and useless.

Ja, that was a shame.

She leaned down for a closer look. Not much quilting left to do. Only the last two squares and the border. The squares were simple enough to figure. Rose had followed a simple, swirling pattern, making the most of each unique design. But it was impossible to know what she'd planned to do for the border. It was made of a green fabric, sprinkled with pink roses. Not a usual choice for an Amish quilt, although of course, it was easy to understand why she'd chosen it.

She wondered if Eben knew what quilting pattern Rose had intended for the border. Since she'd chosen to use only one fabric, likely she'd intended the quilting to be the star of this section. Lilah toyed with the idea of asking Eben if his wife had ever mentioned her plans.

As quickly as the notion occurred to her, she discarded it. She'd not add to his pain with nosy questions. Taking this last memory of his wife apart and stowing it away was going to be painful enough. Not really the sort of thing anyone should have to do alone.

A memory stirred. When one of her sisters-in-law had given birth to a stillborn baby, Lilah and some other women had left their own tasks to look after her other children and help with the household chores. But while there, they'd also emptied the dresser drawer of tiny clothes, boxed up the baby supplies and carried the boxes and the empty crib to the attic. Her brother Donald had told her later how much easier that had made things for Cora and how they'd appreciated coming home from the hospital to find those heartbreaking tasks already tended to.

She hesitated only a second before striding over to the store's telephone. Before she thought better of it, she punched in the number of a local driver.

"Alicia, I need a quick ride right now, round trip. It shouldn't take you more than a half hour. Are you free? Good. Pick me up at Miller's General Store in ten minutes."

Ten minutes wasn't long. So as soon as she hung up, she went to the quilting corner and got to work.

Two and a half hours later, she had just finished smoothing her favorite quilt over its new rack, when she heard the back door open.

"Lilah?" Eben called from the storeroom. He sounded worried, and she heard the thump of a box being set down—doubtlessly not where it went. Eben might be the nicest man she knew, but he was as messy as the rest of them.

She froze, her heart pounding. *"Ja?"*

"Why are you still here?" Boots thumped across the wooden floor. Eben came through the doorway, halting when he caught sight of her. "Is something wrong? I thought you'd have left long ago."

"I wanted to finish something first."

"Finish what?"

She stepped back wordlessly, and his gaze moved to the transformed quilting corner. She held her breath, waiting for his reaction.

There was no doubt the space looked brighter, cleaner and better. That hadn't been easy to manage. Arranging the trip to collect her quilts from Susie's had been the least of her problems. Cleaning this space after years of neglect— that had been time consuming. But it gleamed now, thanks to a lot of elbow grease and lemon wood polish.

That wasn't the biggest change. Rose's dusty quilt had been removed. Lilah had left the empty frame in place because she didn't have the tools to take it apart. But she'd dusted it well, and she'd draped some of her own quilts over it as artistically as she could. She'd also retrieved the empty display racks from the storeroom, cleaned them and hung the rest of her quilts on those.

Eben stared, his face blank with surprise. It took him a few seconds to speak.

"Where is it?"

She knew, of course, what he meant. "I folded it and put it in the storeroom in a bag I found. But—"

"I told you I'd take care of it."

Her heart clenched at the pain in his voice. "I know, but I thought—"

He sighed, raggedly. "I told you as plain as I knew how, Lilah. Rose's quilt was mine to see to. Taking it down, putting it away…that was the last thing I could do for her."

She'd made a mistake. Lilah's hands had started to tremble, and she clasped them firmly in front of her apron. "I'm sorry, Eben. I was only trying to help. I thought maybe it would be easier for you if it was all done. I'm sorry," she repeated miserably.

He didn't say that she was forgiven, that it was all right. He didn't even look at her. His eyes were fixed on the empty quilting frame.

"Eben…"

"Go home, Lilah," he said wearily. "Just go home."

Eben lost track of how long he'd been sitting in the quilting corner after Lilah left.

For a long time, he couldn't think clearly. He just sat, feeling an echo of the same stunned sadness he'd felt after Rose's death.

He'd wanted to take the quilt down himself. He'd put it in the frame for her, all those years ago. The quilt had belonged to Rose, and he should have been the one to fold it up and put it away, not Lilah. Especially given the new gossip that was going around.

If folks hadn't been saying such things before, they certain sure would be now. Eben felt guilty—and frustrated. He knew Lilah had meant well, but he wished for once she'd simply followed his instructions.

But as the minutes ticked by, his troubled feelings faded, and he noticed some things.

A fresh scent, clean and lemony, hung in the air. Lilah must have done some serious scrubbing. He hadn't realized until this minute how musty this area had become. It was a nice change, that.

It wasn't the only one. There were new quilts, hanging around the room and draped over the frame. Lilah's quilts made the space feel a lot brighter and warmer. It took him a minute to figure out why.

She didn't favor light colors in her sewing. She'd chosen materials of deep, rich shades, not the softer pinks and blues that Rose had liked.

He walked slowly around, studying each quilt in turn. He was no expert on sewing, but he recognized good workmanship when he saw it. And he'd been a storekeeper long enough to know instinctively what was likely to sell well in his store.

These would sell, and for a good price, too.

That was the most important thing, of course. Whether he liked the quilts himself or not didn't matter. You stocked them for the customers, not for yourself.

But, the truth was, he did like them.

He liked the bold, steady colors, the decisive designs. There was nothing delicate about them. He reached out to finger a corner of the nearest one thoughtfully. It wasn't just the designs. Lilah had used sturdy materials that wouldn't tear easily, nor fray.

He liked that. There was nothing here to fuss or worry over because these quilts weren't made for show. *Nee*, they were made to last, for a family to live with and to use. They could be smoothed every morning over beds or tucked around sleeping children while snow fell outside. They would hold up for years. Over time, with many washings, they might grow a bit softer, a little faded, but they would hold together.

A customer might pay a steep price for a quilt like this, but still they'd get themselves a real *gut* bargain.

He'd been too short with Lilah about taking Rose's quilt down. He felt a flush of shame. She'd clearly been worried, sorry to have overstepped and upset him. He shouldn't have spoken so sharp. Of course, she hadn't understood how he'd feel. How could she? And the gossip he was fretting over wasn't her fault, either.

He'd need to apologize, first thing tomorrow. But tonight, he'd better spend some time praying that *Gott* would give him the right words to say and some guidance about how to handle the firestorm of gossip that was surely coming. He sure couldn't afford to dig this hole any deeper.

The following morning, he was waiting in the storeroom when Lilah came to work. She shot him a wary glance as she walked in.

"Good morning, Eben." She set down her lunch cooler, which looked heavy. She must have packed another big lunch for them all today, even though he'd not been very kind last night.

That made him feel even worse.

"Lilah," he said—and stopped. He'd practiced what he needed to say all the way over here this morning in the buggy, but every well-chosen word had gone right out of his head.

She had paused in the act of untying her black bonnet, waiting for him to speak. He had to say something.

"I'm sorry," he blurted out. "I was short with you over the quilt, and I shouldn't have been. I hope you'll forgive me."

"There's nothing to forgive," she said quickly, that little pucker forming over her brow. "I was the one in the wrong. I shouldn't have taken it out of the frame. I meant well, but Susie and I talked it over, and she helped me to understand why it was important for you to tend to that yourself. I should be apologizing to you."

"*Nee*, it was my fault. I shouldn't have been so upset. But that quilt…it was special. It was meant to tell a story—our story, mine and Rose's. Each square was a memory, something we'd shared together." He shifted, uncomfortably. It was hard, talking about such things. "She was making it for me, so I wouldn't forget the happy times we'd had together."

"That is a beautiful idea. I'm sorry she never got to finish it. Maybe we could put my quilts in some other part of the store." Her brow furrowed as she thought this over. "We could rearrange some things, if that would be easier on you."

"That's a kind thought, but I'd rather leave things as they are. I like the way you've fixed things up."

Her eyes searched his. Plainly, she was unconvinced. "Are you sure?"

"*Ja*, I'm sure. But, Lilah—" He paused, wondering if he should warn her about the gossip that was starting. But surely she'd know herself that people were talking. Women seemed to pick up on such things quickly. Even as ill as she was, Rose had always known the local news—who was courting, whose marriage was about to be published, that sort of thing—well before he had any idea himself.

Lilah lifted an eyebrow. "What, Eben?"

"Nothing. I'm happy we got things straightened out."

"Me, too." Something in her tone caught his attention, a soft shyness he hadn't heard before. But when she caught him looking at her, she blinked and turned away to fuss over hanging up her bonnet. "You're no treat to work with when you're grumpy."

Eben was smiling as he went to unlock the door.

That smile didn't last too long, though. He wasn't wrong about the gossip.

It started when Emma Hershberger, the local woman who put together the baking mixes for him, stopped by to deliver a new order. When she saw the new quilts, her eyes widened—but she said nothing. However, the next day, her two *kossins* came in—and they'd never set foot in his store before. During the rest of the week, half a dozen other Plain women suddenly found reasons to drop by Miller's General Store. Several more stayed outside but peeped through the window, using their hands to shade against the glare.

By Saturday afternoon, he wished they'd all stay outside. The women who came in the store weren't any too subtle, either. Lots of knowing looks and little side-smiles came his way.

That was annoying.

But what was even more annoying was that he couldn't tell what Lilah thought about it—or if she'd even noticed. She answered the women's questions cheerfully, but if she'd guessed why they were so interested in quilts all of a sudden, she did a *gut* job of hiding it.

It was even worse at church on Sunday. Wives had obviously spoken to their husbands, and Eben was winked at and slapped on the back more times than he could count.

Plainly, the whole community was convinced he and Lilah were on their way to the altar, and he still had no idea what Lilah thought about it all. She went about her business as matter-of-factly as ever. The Stoltzfus family was hosting church, and she stayed busy helping Arlena Stoltzfus and her daughters. Eben kept his distance, watching as she helped serve lunch and clean up, working with her usual quiet efficiency.

Had she figured out what people were saying about the two of them? If she did know, did she mind?

He couldn't tell, and for some reason, he very much wanted to know. And if he could get her alone for a minute or two, he figured he'd find out how she felt right quick. Lilah wasn't one to mince her words, and she was never shy about stating an opinion.

But it wasn't until well after lunch, when people were loading their families back into the buggies to go home, that he saw an opening. Lilah was carrying some empty dishes out to Susie Raber's buggy when he came up beside her.

"I think we should talk."

She stopped in the yard, looking startled. "All right. What about?"

"Not here." He glanced uneasily at the house. There were only a few families left, and nobody seemed to be paying them any attention, but this was a conversation best had in private. "Let's go around back of the barn."

"Why can't we talk here?" She frowned. "Susie's nearly ready to leave."

"It'll only take a minute." He took the dishes out of her hand and set them on the buggy seat. "Come on."

"All right, but we'll have to be quick." She followed him around the side of the barn. "What is it?"

He drew in a deep breath—and had no idea what to say. He should have thought this through.

Do you know everybody thinks we're courting? And if you do know, do you mind having your name coupled up with mine like that?

He couldn't ask her that, could he?

"You know," Lilah said suddenly, "there's something I want to talk to you about, too. I've just been too *naerfich* to bring it up."

Relief flooded him. So, she had noticed the gossip swirling around them—and now, Lilah-like, she was going to tell him exactly what she thought about it.

"Don't be *naerfich*," he said gently. "If there's something you need to talk to me about, go ahead." He held his breath.

"All right." She paused. "You should let me wash Rose's quilt."

The breath he was holding whooshed out. "What?"

"I know." She held up one hand as if to stop his argument.

"It's very personal, and all that. I'm truly not trying to stick my nose where it doesn't belong again, but something so special shouldn't be put away dirty. It's going to be ruined, and you don't want that. It'll be tricky to clean because it's not finished, but I'll do my best. If you'll let me. Will you?"

"I—" He didn't know what to say. "*Ja*. Sure. I'd appreciate that."

"*Gut*." She nodded. "Drop it off at Susie's, and I'll see to it. It'll take some time, though, because I'll have to be real careful."

"I know you will, and there's no rush. But I should pay you for the help."

"*Nee*." She shook her head firmly. "I offered. You will not pay me anything."

He thought of arguing, then decided against it. "*Denki*, Lilah. You're being very kind."

"You're welcome." She shrugged, her eyes meeting his in that honest, level way she had. "It's no great thing to wash a quilt, although this one will be more trouble than most."

He liked that. No silly fluttering, no pretending, no saying one thing and meaning something else. Just Lilah being herself, like always.

"Now we've got that settled," she said, "what did you want to talk to me about?"

She didn't know about the gossip, he decided. She wouldn't be acting like this if she did—as if it were any ordinary day. He'd have to think of some way to warn her, so she wouldn't be caught off guard by it.

The problem was, it was hard to think just now with her standing so close to him, her head tilted ever so slightly to one side as she looked up into his face.

She had real pretty eyes, Lilah did. Brown but with sprinkles of green mixed in.

He'd never really noticed that before. And she smelled like cookies and flowers, like lots of sweet things all mixed together.

"Eben?" Her voice lilted up on his name. "Was there something you wanted?"

"Ja." He leaned down as he spoke, and her eyes widened, searching his.

But she didn't move away.

"There you are," a deep voice boomed behind them. "We were wondering where you two had disappeared to."

Their bishop, Charley Coblentz, stood at the corner of the barn. His face was solemn, but there was a knowing twinkle in his blue eyes. No doubt Charley had heard the gossip going around and thought he'd interrupted some romantic moment.

It didn't help that he felt as dumbstruck and guilty as if he had been caught stealing a kiss.

Maybe he almost had been.

"Lilah," Charley went on in a kindly tone, "Susie is looking for you. She's ready to leave."

"Oh, of course. I'd better go. *Mach's gut*, Charley. And Eben." Lilah hurried around the corner of the barn and out of sight.

Eben watched her go, envying her the escape. No doubt he was in for a lecture.

And no doubt he deserved it. It had been his idea to sneak off behind the barn. He turned back to Charley and braced himself for a sermon on seemly behavior.

"Well," the bishop said. "It's high time. Everybody thinks so."

Eben blinked. He hadn't been on the receiving end of one of these lectures since he was a teenager, but they couldn't have changed this much.

"High time?" Eben's Sunday clothes suddenly felt too hot. "Charley, Lilah and I… We're not…"

Charley held up a hand, interrupting him. "*Ja, ja*, I know. It's early days yet, much too early for folks to be interfering. But I just wanted you to know how pleased we are—all of us. It's what we've all been praying for. You've lingered in your grief so long, and that's not a wise thing." Charley clapped Eben on the back. "But maybe don't go sneaking off behind barns, *ja*? At least not until you're man and wife."

"Charley?" A woman's voice called from the yard. "Where are you?"

"I'm coming, Martha!" The older man gave Eben a wink. "High time," he repeated.

Then he walked back around the barn to join his wife.

Chapter Twelve

Instead of going back into the kitchen, where Susie was waiting, Lilah hurried across the yard and ducked behind the Stoltzfus chicken coop. She leaned against the planks of the small building, one hand pressed over her pounding heart, trying to collect her scattered wits.

What had just—almost—happened?

When the bishop had popped up behind them, she'd felt...caught. As if the two of them had stolen away together on purpose, like a courting couple so sweet on each other they couldn't go an afternoon without a moment alone.

Which, of course, they weren't, so she shouldn't have felt strange at all. She'd only offered to wash a dirty quilt for him, and it was hard to think of anything less romantic than that.

But there at the last, when he'd looked into her eyes... Just for a second, she'd thought Eben was about to kiss her. And she wouldn't have minded a bit—not one little bit—if he had.

She wasn't sure which of those two things surprised her the most.

Her heartbeat, which had been slowing, jumped back into a gallop at the memory. She began to pace behind the coop, careful to stay out of sight of the house.

When, exactly, had she started feeling this way about Eben? She wasn't sure. The change had sneaked up on her, little by little. She'd known she liked him, of course, that she respected him, that she enjoyed his company. But this...

This was different.

And for a minute there, when they'd been looking at each other, it sure had seemed like Eben was feeling different about her, too.

It had seemed so. But could it be that she was misreading things? After all, she'd been mistaken about Eben before. No doubt she was wrong again, and he'd had no idea of kissing her. Besides, she'd never been kissed in her life, so what did she know about it? Nothing, that was what.

"Charley!"

Lilah froze as Martha Coblentz called from the back steps of the house. The bishop's answer was muffled, but a minute later, he walked around the barn. He and his wife started across the yard in Lilah's direction, headed to where their buggy was waiting, the horse hitched up and ready.

Lilah shrank back against the coop. She couldn't very well pop out now with no explanation of why she was lurking around the chickens. Better to wait for the Coblentz buggy to leave. Then she'd go find Susie.

"What were you doing behind the barn?" Martha asked her husband as they walked together.

Charley chuckled. "Being a spoilsport. A couple had stolen off for a few minutes alone."

"Lilah Troyer and Eben Miller, I'm guessing." A delighted laugh. "I see by your face I'm right. The women could talk of nothing else in the kitchen, although Susie did what she could to quiet it. There's a divided opinion on whether Lilah's getting her hopes up for nothing or Eben's finally thinking of marrying again."

"Mind your step there, Martha. Going by what I saw just now, I'd say the ones expecting a wedding have the right of it."

"Oh, my!" Lilah clapped her hand over her mouth, afraid the bishop and his wife had heard her. However, the chickens clucking must have hidden the noise because the couple continued their conversation.

A wedding? So that was why people had been looking at her funny all day? Because they thought she and Eben were a couple?

If she—and the bishop—hadn't been mistaken, then maybe…could it really be? Lilah's heart was hammering so hard now she could hear her pulse in her ears.

"Well, that's good news, I suppose." The buggy creaked as Martha hoisted herself into it.

"You suppose?" the bishop responded. "Why wouldn't it be good news?"

Lilah frowned and leaned as far around the coop as she dared, hoping to hear the answer.

"Oh, it's certainly good news for Lilah. She'll jump at him, I'm sure, and who could blame her, poor thing. She's near twice the age of most of our girls when they marry. Being Eben's wife will mean a far better life for her than she could have hoped for."

"It'll be good for Eben, too. He's been alone far too long."

"That's true. He was such a devoted husband to Rose. Most men wouldn't have looked twice at a girl with so many health problems, but he's got a soft heart, our Eben does. No doubt that's what's behind this. He feels sorry for Lilah. And he does well enough at that store of his to keep them both comfortable. But—"

"But what?" Another creak as Charley took his own seat. "I still don't see what the trouble is."

"Oh, there's no trouble. Except…"

"Except what?" The bishop demanded impatiently.

"Well, you know how *gut* Eben is with the little ones. They flock to him like kittens to a bowl of milk. A man like that should have a big family of his own, don't you think? Plenty of younger girls have cast looks at our Eben. He could have his pick. Lots of widowers do that, marry young wives and start new families. And Lilah…she's a real hard worker and a faithful church member, but she must be at least forty by now." A heavy sigh, followed by the gentle slap of reins on a horse's back.

Charley said something that Lilah couldn't hear. The buggy rolled toward the road and out of earshot.

She walked out from behind the coop, suddenly not caring anymore who saw her.

So, she'd jump at Eben's offer of marriage, would she? But he'd be making a bad bargain, marrying someone like her, someone he felt sorry for. Even though she was…what had Martha said? A hard worker and a faithful church member.

Those were good things to be, of course. But she suspected they weren't the first things most men thought of when they were looking for a bride. And as Martha said, Eben could easily choose someone younger. Someone who could give him a dozen children to love.

And for a man like Eben, that would be the most important thing. He deserved a family of his own, sons and daughters to care for, who would help him with the business as he aged and who would give him grandchildren someday.

He deserved far more than a blunt-spoken old *maidel* like her could give him.

Lilah collected Susie from the kitchen, ignoring the sidelong looks and smiles she got from the other three women who'd stayed to help put the house to rights. As soon as they reached home, she said she wasn't feeling well and retreated to the privacy of her bedroom, refusing Susie's kind offer to brew a pot of peppermint tea.

It wouldn't have done her a bit of good. Tea did wonders for an upset stomach or a headache, but it was not much good at curing wounded pride—or selfishness.

And those were the battles she would be fighting tonight.

Eben went in to work early on Monday morning. He figured he might as well. He'd woken up well before his usual time and hadn't been able to get back to sleep.

That had happened before, of course, many times. In those first months after Rose's death, he'd spent plenty of hours awake in the dark emptiness of his house, alone with his memories.

Over time, his misery had gentled into a familiar, quiet sadness. He'd grown accustomed to it, like he'd grown used to how the arm he'd broken as a *youngie* ached when the weather shifted to cold.

But this morning felt different.

Instead of lingering in the past, today his thoughts kept drifting toward the future, turning over possibilities so fragile and strange that they had his belly tied in a knot. Because the more he thought about these things, the more he wanted them.

He tried to tell himself he was being silly, that he'd allowed the gossip and the bishop to put ideas in his head that had no business there. But finally, on the ride in to work in the balmy darkness of a predawn summer morning, he faced the truth.

He liked the idea of a future with Lilah—and he desperately wanted to know if Lilah might feel the same way about him. One thing was for sure—she'd tell him, one way or the other. Lilah wasn't the sort who left a fellow guessing.

He took some extra time to settle Blaze comfortably in the stable where he rented a stall. Even so, he unlocked the store well over an hour early, just as the dawn lightened the skies, casting a warm glow over the silent building.

He shut the door behind himself, turning the lock against any early-bird customers. But then, instead of starting his usual first-thing-in-the-morning routine, he stood where he was and gave Miller's General Store a good look-over.

Things sure had changed.

Before, he'd walked into a musty-smelling store every day with a weary sense of being overwhelmed. He never seemed to come to the end of the tasks that waited for him, no matter how hard he tried.

But now, each morning the store waited, ready for a busy day. It was always neat and organized, the shelves well stocked. The smell of lemon wood polish hung pleasantly in the air, mingling with the scents of candles and baking spices.

Ja, everything was different now. Everything was better.

It wasn't just the store. He was better, himself. All thanks to Lilah.

He glanced toward the quilting corner, his eyes lingering on the cheerful colors. Lilah's quilts were so much like her. Bright and beautiful and strong.

He liked that a lot. He liked her—a lot.

The question was, how did she feel about him?

He wanted to find out the answer to that question. He wanted to know if there was any possibility that the talk swirling around the two of them might prove to be more than empty gossip.

He was pretty sure she liked him at least a little better

than she had to start with. She wasn't near as stiff around him as she'd been at the first, and her smiles sure came a lot easier—more often, too.

But Lilah, as she'd pointed out a long while ago, wasn't like Rose. Rose had been sweet, delicate and clinging. Fresh out of her teens when they'd married, she'd arranged her life and her opinions around his, depending on him for everything.

Lilah was nothing like that. She was opinionated and independent. Even though she'd said that being unmarried had been no choice of hers, he wondered if deep down she didn't enjoy her single life. Would she really want to change that, if she was given the opportunity?

Especially if the opportunity came with his name on it.

That was the question that had cost him a night's sleep and gotten him to the store so early. Now he just had to figure out some way to find out the answer.

He walked back to the storeroom to hang up his hat and unlock the back door so that Lilah could come in that way, as she usually did. And then he settled in to wait.

Whatever Lilah was thinking, it didn't impact her morning routine. The back door opened exactly at her usual time. Eben immediately dropped the bill he'd been trying to look over and headed for the storeroom.

She was untying her black bonnet as he walked in, and she glanced up at him, startled.

"Eben. *Gut mariye.*"

"Good morning, Lilah," he responded automatically— and then he stood awkwardly by as she hung her bonnet on its peg and stowed her lunch cooler on its usual shelf.

He wasn't sure what to say. It had been years since he'd liked a girl, since he'd had to fish a bit to find out if she liked him back. And since he'd settled on Rose early on, he'd not done much of that, even back in the day.

But, of course, for the young folks, it was simpler. Every teenaged boy knew how to spark up a courtship. You'd make some conversation with the girl you liked, and if she seemed friendly enough, you'd take the risk of asking her to ride home with you from a singing. If she said yes once, that meant you had a chance. If she said yes a second time, you were usually off and running. Courtships were kept quiet, but there was no secret to them. Everybody knew the steps to take.

But this was different. He and Lilah were grown adults, and he'd paid little attention to how courtships were handled at this stage of life. After Rose's death, he'd had no interest in it.

Until now.

Lilah was studying him with narrowed eyes. "What is it, Eben? Is there something you'd like to say?"

A perfectly ordinary question, but he'd grown to know Lilah pretty well. He noticed an oddness in her voice, and the way she lifted her chin as she spoke. She knew perfectly well that something was up.

This was the moment to ask her—something. The problem was, he wasn't sure what he should ask. So he blurted out the first thing that came to mind.

"Would you like to go for a ride one afternoon with me?"

She frowned. "You mean like out to the Fishers?"

"*Ja*, sure, there." Or anywhere else she wanted to go, but he wasn't sure how to get that across. He was bumbling this. Apparently, flirting with girls wasn't something a man got better at with time. He'd been much smoother as a *youngie*.

"Do you want me to look over some more things they want you to sell?" Lilah seemed uneasy, and she wasn't meeting his eyes. "If you're asking for my opinion, I think it's too soon for that. We've not seen how well the things I picked out last time will do. Besides, we've hardly any room to put new items. Maybe later, when you've seen what's selling well and what isn't. Speaking of that, I wanted to get the new Amish dolls Ruth Fisher made out before we open this morning. I'm hoping they'll be real popular."

With that, she picked up a small box of the faceless dolls and brushed past him into the store area. This morning she smelled of vanilla, cinnamon and coffee. Like a cozy breakfast in a warm kitchen.

Eben stayed where he was, trying to think.

That had not gone the way he'd hoped. Obviously, Lilah had no idea how close he'd come to kissing her yesterday. She still didn't know he was interested in more than friendship with her. He'd think it through and try again, smarter this time.

The trouble was, he wasn't sure exactly how to go about that.

He mulled it over throughout the day as they worked. There were a good many customers, so they were both kept busy. Lilah's quilts were attracting a lot of attention, and she spent a fair amount of time answering questions about them. One woman asked for a quilt to be custom-made. Lilah made notes on the back of a discarded envelope about what all the lady wanted.

Eben eavesdropped shamelessly, and he held his breath when Lilah prepared to quote the lady a price. He needn't have worried. The amount she gave was fair, both for her and for the customer.

Ja, he thought proudly, Lilah was smart as well as talented with her needle. She had plenty of common sense, and she was honest as a new penny. A hard worker, too, with a brisk, cheerful energy that made workdays pleasant.

In fact, the longer he watched her that day the more he wondered how she'd ended up on the shelf in the first place. Lilah would make a fine wife for any man.

Sure, she spoke her mind plainly, but in Eben's opinion that was a pleasant change from having to guess at a woman's thoughts and feelings. And she'd never been the showiest looking *maidel*, but she had a simple prettiness that he liked better anyhow. He liked the smooth darkness of her hair and the strong line of her jaw—and that sprinkle of unexpected green in her eyes.

Ja, it was the unexpectedness of Lilah that he liked best.

He and Corey spent the late afternoon mounting some shelves on the wall to make more space for the new stock. Normally, he'd have waited until after closing to do such a task, but the boy liked to help.

Eben liked it, too. It was pleasant, teaching Corey how to use tools correctly, how to make sure the shelves were straight and strong. The boy learned fast and worked hard, too—and best of all, there'd been no more instances of stealing.

Today, though, Eben was distracted. As they worked, he darted glances at Lilah, waiting on customers at the counter. She was wearing a dark green dress today, and he privately thought she looked very nice.

"*Onkel* Eben?" Corey said, trying his best to say the *Deutsch* word correctly. They'd lit on that title since Eben felt uncomfortable being called "Mr. Eben." It sounded too fancy. Plain children usually called adults simply by their first names, but since *Englisch* children didn't, this had seemed a good compromise.

Eben smiled at the boy around the screws he held in his

mouth, momentarily distracted from his thoughts about Lilah. He spat the screws into his hand so he could speak.

"What?"

"You got some extra jobs I could do? I want to earn up some store credit."

"Could be. What are you needing the credit for?"

The boy shot a look at his sister. She was sitting on a stool beside Lilah, playing quietly with one of the new Amish dolls. "Bethany's birthday is coming up. She really likes that doll, so I'm gonna get it for her."

Eben had been planning to give Bethany the doll anyhow, and he started to say so. But then he noticed the determination on Corey's freckled face, and he paused to consider.

The whole point of this was to help build the boy's character. Giving him things wouldn't do that. Letting him earn them might.

"Ja," he said thoughtfully. "I think we could work that out between us. I figure you've just about paid off the items you took before. If you want to keep on helping out here—"

"I do!"

"Then we'll have to work out something that's fair to both of us. This seems a fair trade, a few hours of work for the doll. Since you've been working so hard here, I will let you have the doll for what I paid for it myself." He quoted a price and had the satisfaction of seeing Corey's face light up.

"That's a real good deal."

"Then we're agreed. Work here the rest of the week, and that doll will be yours by the weekend."

Corey stuck out his hand, and Eben shook it solemnly.

"It's kind of you," he said. "Doing this for your sister."

The boy shrugged, looking pleased and embarrassed. "She's little, so she likes things like that. But don't say anything about it, okay? I want it to be a surprise. Girls really like surprises. And presents." Corey nodded sagely.

"Most of them do, *ja*." Eben's eyes strayed over to Lilah, who had bent down to whisper something to Bethany. Both of them laughed, and he found himself smiling, even though he didn't know what they were so happy about.

The smile lingered even as he turned back to the shelves. Because Corey had reminded him of something he'd almost forgotten. Most girls did like presents and surprises.

And that gave him an idea…

Chapter Thirteen

The following Friday was the day Lilah had decided to re-organize the baking mixes, but instead of focusing on her task, she was watching Anna Speicher out of the corner of her eye. The young widow had brought her baby son into the store over twenty minutes ago, but she'd not bought anything, nor even picked anything up. She'd just walked around, bouncing Matthew in her arms.

Lilah didn't think she was really here to shop at all.

Anna seemed nervous, and she kept darting uneasy glances in Eben's direction. Two or three times, she'd started to go to the counter where he was working. But then a customer would walk up, and she'd stop where she was, pretending to look at the items on whatever shelf was closest by.

Her *mamm* wasn't with her, but Lilah suspected Mary Glick was behind this visit, just the same. Clearly Anna would rather have been anywhere else.

Still, she seemed to have taken a *gut* bit of trouble over her looks. She was wearing a dress in a deep lavender color, and her son's little shirt was cut from the same cloth. The little boy looked adorable, and the color suited Anna's fair coloring real well, too.

That was no accident, Lilah thought irritably, then felt ashamed of herself. Envy was a sin, and there was nothing more mean-spirited that resenting someone else's happiness simply because you wished you could have it for yourself.

Not that Anna looked too happy just yet. In fact, she looked as if she might throw up. But once she got her courage up and actually spoke to Eben—if she ever did—likely she'd catch his eye, just as her *mamm* hoped. Especially with her little son cuddled in her arms—Eben was so softhearted about children. Matthew had turned one not too long ago, and he was a cute child with wide blue eyes and wispy blond hair.

Eben's heart couldn't hold out long against these two. And that, Lilah assured herself sternly, was a very *gut* thing. If he married Anna, he'd have himself a ready-made family. Even Martha Coblentz would have no doubts about such a marriage, Lilah was certain.

Smothering a sigh, she moved a few calico bags of apple cinnamon bread mix off the shelf and into a box. She'd be putting these on the discount table. High summer wasn't a time when people hankered for apple cinnamon treats— these should've been ordered for the fall. In their place, she arranged mixes for lemon bars and something called a chocolate picnic cake. Those were the sorts of goodies people wanted to bake in the summertime.

Right now, she herself didn't much like the idea of baking anything. It was hot in the store this early afternoon, and she was feeling annoyed. Today had been an unsettling day.

Not only because of Anna, although Lilah did wish the other woman would just speak to Eben and get it over with. Eben himself seemed restless and preoccupied, and he kept glancing at the clock as if he was expecting something.

He'd been acting odd all week, but not for the reason she'd expected.

When he'd popped into the storeroom the minute she'd arrived at work on Monday, she'd felt sure he was going to bring up that moment behind the barn—or maybe the gossip that was going around about the two of them.

She'd hoped he wouldn't.

He might make some sort of apology, letting her know he didn't have any such feelings for her, an embarrassing reminder of what had happened back in their school days. Once again, Lilah would be the awkward, unwanted girl who had to be told to her face that a fellow wasn't interested.

Sadly, that was the better of the two options.

Because if Eben really had been about to kiss her behind the barn on Sunday, she was facing an even bigger problem. Not because she didn't feel the same way about him.

But because she did.

But Eben had hardly said anything at all—except something about them taking a ride together. And when she'd sidestepped that, he'd seemed perfectly happy to let it go. He'd not suggested anything like it again, so he must not have been so interested in her after all.

Which should have been a relief and certainly shouldn't have stung as much as it had. She ought to be used to being overlooked by now.

People had only started gossiping because they'd noticed a change in Eben. After three years, he was finally coming out of his grief.

That was a very *gut* thing.

The man worked far too hard. He needed a wife to fuss over him, someone who'd make sure he ate well and rested enough. And anybody watching him with Corey and Bethany could also see that he needed children, too, just as much.

Ja, that was what he needed, and sooner or later he'd

know it himself. Unless his loneliness pushed him to make a poor choice. Someone he felt sorry for, maybe. Someone everyone knew could never really make a man like Eben Miller happy.

Lilah thunked another pretty yellow cloth bag on the shelf.

"Lilah? Could I speak with you a minute?"

She turned to find Anna looking at her, her blue eyes wide and worried. Matthew blinked owlishly at Lilah from his mother's arms.

Lilah tweaked the baby's nose and was rewarded with a smile. "*Ja*, but I'm not the one you really want to speak to, am I? It's clear there's something on your mind and that you're wanting to talk to Eben. Why don't you stop dithering and just go speak to him?"

Anna looked taken aback for a second, but then she nodded.

"You're right. The truth is, I need to ask Eben a favor, and I…don't like doing it."

Lilah sighed. "I wouldn't be too *naerfich* about that if I were you. What is it you need?"

"I need to…sell some of my belongings. Some furniture and other household things. I was wondering if Eben might let me put a paper up here, advertising what's for sale and the prices and all."

The other girl looked so embarrassed that Lilah's heart went out to her. She could guess what Anna wasn't saying and why Mary was so anxious for her daughter to find another husband. Money was tight now that her husband's farming income was gone, and the widow needed to sell some things to get by. *Englischers* would be likelier to pay a high price for such things, so it was a *schmaert* move to put the fliers in a store like this one.

"I don't see any other advertisements up, so I wasn't sure Eben would allow it," Anna was saying. "I've been trying to catch him alone because I didn't want him to feel bad about saying no."

"Oh, he's not going to say no. He almost never does. Wait here." Lilah strode over to the counter, where for some reason an *Englisch* lady was telling Eben about her stomach problems as he rang up her order. "*Excuse mich.* I'm very sorry to interrupt, but you're needed, Eben. Anna there needs to speak to you. I'll take care of this."

Eben flashed her a grateful look and made his apologies. As he walked over to speak with Anna—pausing to tickle Matthew's chin—Lilah couldn't help but think what a nice-looking family they would make. Matthew was such a cute little fellow, and Anna had a gentle personality, much like Rose's. Mary was right. This would be a good match.

After the customer left, Lilah glanced over to the corner of the store where Anna and Eben were still talking. Anna looked up at him, her child nestled sleepily against her shoulder, her face glowing with relief. Eben must have agreed to put the sales flyers up—but of course, Lilah had known he would.

Eben was speaking to her earnestly, his expression gentle. Of course, he would know just what to say because he could understand how Anna was feeling. After all, he had lost his partner, too, maybe not so unexpectedly as Anna, but still far too soon.

Another reason why the two of them would be a good pair. Those were adding up. Susie should have nudged Anna and Eben together from the start. How silly of her to ever think that he could be seriously interested in someone like Lilah instead.

How silly of anybody to think such a thing.

Lilah rummaged under the counter for a dust rag and the can of polish she'd stowed there. She scrubbed the wooden surface with brisk, hard strokes, forcing herself to focus on the work and not look back over toward Eben and Anna.

She was successful enough that she was startled when Eben walked up to the counter a few minutes later.

"Thanks for taking over," he said. "That took a little longer than it should have."

"It was no problem," Lilah said stiffly. "I suppose you've agreed to put up her flyers, then?"

"*Ja*, of course. And I told her we would clear off a table so she could sell some of the smaller things she has. Dishes and such that she doesn't need."

"Where are we going to put those? The store's over-crowded as it is." Lilah winced at the sharpness in her own voice. She was letting her envy get the best of her again— and if she wasn't careful, Eben would figure that out.

But he only gave her a puzzled look and shrugged. "We'll do one small table. I'm sure we can fit that in some-place. Anyway, I don't expect the items will last long. You know how *Englischers* love to buy secondhand things from Plain people."

He was right, of course. About all of it. And she was being mean-spirited. "*Ja*, that's true. It's kind of you to help her. Just let me know what you'd like me to do."

"There won't be much. She's going to put the prices on before she brings them, and we'll just need to keep that money separate." He glanced toward the door, and his eyes lit up. "The school bus is stopping. Corey and Beth-any are here."

"They'll be hungry, like always." She put the polish away. "I'll go set their snacks out on the storeroom table."

Eben walked behind the counter. "It's real kind of you to

bring us all food every day. I'd like to start helping. I know you have the extra bread and sweets that Susie gets from the bakery, but maybe I could buy some fruit to round things out. Apples and oranges, things like that."

"*Ja*, that would be nice."

He sighed, looking through the store windows at Corey helping Bethany down the bus steps. "I'd do a lot more for them, if I could."

"Me, too."

"I know." To her astonishment, he reached over and patted her arm. "You're a very kindhearted woman, Lilah Troyer."

She flushed hot. If he only knew…

"Hi, *Onkel* Eben!" Bethany threw open the door and ran across the store, her fraying pigtails flying. Lilah had braided those herself—two days ago. Obviously nobody had washed or combed the little girl's hair since. And that faded pink shirt she was wearing was at least a size too small.

Lilah pressed her lips together tightly. Those foster parents needed to pay closer attention. She didn't know much about how that system worked, but surely someone would want to know how little care these children were getting.

But at least the smile on Bethany's face was beautiful, and Eben matched it with one of his own. He gave her a big hug. "It's good to see you, little one."

"Are you ready for your snack?" Lilah bent down to accept her own hug, relishing the feel of the child's arms around her neck.

"Bethany, you go ahead and eat," Eben suggested. "But if Corey wouldn't mind waiting for his snack for a few minutes, I could use his help. Lilah, can you keep an eye on the customers? We'll have to leave the store for a little while."

"Of course," Lilah agreed immediately, but she was curious. It was unlike Eben to leave the store for any length of time during the day.

"Can I come, too?" Bethany asked.

"No," Corey told his sister. "This is something secret me and *Onkel* Eben have to see about. You have to stay here."

"That's not fair." Bethany looked disappointed at being left out, and Lilah felt a sneaking sympathy.

A secret? Lilah was more curious than ever—and a little hurt that Eben hadn't shared this with her as he'd obviously done with Corey. But likely it was some sort of surprise they'd fixed up for Bethany's upcoming birthday, and that shouldn't be spoiled.

"That's all right. You'll get first pick of the cookies today," she told the little girl cheerfully. "And I brought some extra nice ones."

"Cookies? Yay! Okay, *Onkel* Eben. I'll stay here with—" Bethany paused and frowned. "How do you say *aunt*? In the funny way you talk?"

"Bethany!" Corey shot his sister an agonized look.

"Aent," Eben supplied before Lilah could answer.

"I'll stay here with *Aent* Lilah," Bethany finished happily.

Corey looked at Lilah uneasily. "You can't just go calling people stuff. *Onkel* Eben told us to call him that, but Lilah didn't. She might not like it. We ain't really family."

Eben had told the children to call him that, although Amish children usually only referred to their relatives by their first names. He'd explained to Lilah that he'd figured these little ones would feel more comfortable using the titles, since *Englisch* children spoke of their relatives so.

"I know we're not a real family." Bethany's smile faded. "I just like to pretend we are while we're here."

"That's all right," Lilah assured the little girl quickly. "I don't mind. I'd be real happy to be your *aent*."

"Good!" Bethany said. She sighed. "I wish we could be a real family. Me and Corey and you and *Onkel* Eben."

"I do, too."

At the sound of her own words, Lilah froze. She couldn't believe she'd said what she'd been thinking right out loud. She hadn't meant to, but her heart had been so full of the same exact wish that Bethany was talking about that the words had just popped out.

Horrified, she glanced up at Eben. He looked back, his blue-gray eyes twinkling with amusement—and something else, too. She wasn't sure what it was, but it made her cheeks heat up even more.

"I'm sorry," she murmured in *Deutsch*. "I wasn't thinking… I didn't mean…"

"Go fix Bethany a snack," he said in English. "Corey and I won't be gone long."

Lilah nodded mutely—she didn't dare say another word—and taking Bethany by the hand, she retreated hastily into the storeroom.

Later that afternoon, Eben glanced up at the clock and almost groaned out loud. That minute hand didn't seem to be moving at all. There were still ten minutes left until closing time.

After he and Corey returned to the store following their errand, the rest of the afternoon dragged. He couldn't wait for the workday to be over so he could show Lilah the surprise he'd had made for her.

Corey's remark about girls liking unexpected gifts had sparked the idea. Because—although Eben hadn't courted in years—he knew Corey was right. Women did appreciate such things, so it was common for young fellows to give little tokens to girls they had their eyes on.

Not too often and nothing big, usually, because there wasn't much money to spend. But small things. A carving, maybe, whittled from a piece of wood in the evenings. A paper bag of her favorite candy. A flower or two snitched from a mother's garden. He'd done those things himself as a *youngie*, partly because they did make girls smile.

And more importantly, because they sent a message. *I like you. I think you're special.*

The fact that he felt that way about Lilah was something he was still struggling to wrap his head around. After Rose's death, he'd never thought he'd care like that about another woman.

But now, he did care—about Lilah.

And once he'd started noticing Lilah that way, he hadn't been able to stop. He noticed things about her every day now, things he liked, such as how sweet her smile was and how her laugh sounded so unexpectedly young and bubbly. He noticed things that made him laugh himself, like her all-too-honest remarks. He found things to worry over, like her tendency to pick up heavy things instead of asking for his help and how she'd fluff up at rude customers like a little bantam hen.

So, *ja*, he thought Lilah was special for certain sure. He just wasn't sure how to tell her so. He was hoping this gift would do that job for him—and maybe even let him know how Lilah felt about him, too. Because—and this was unusual with Lilah—he honestly had no idea.

Sometimes he thought maybe Lilah liked him pretty well. There was a certain way she looked at him, like when she was teasing him or when one of the *kinder* said something funny. Warm and sweet, as if they were sharing a secret together.

And there'd been that little slipup she'd made today, agreeing with Bethany how nice it would be for them all to be a family. That had sent his hopes to the ceiling—until she'd followed it up with an apology.

"*Onkel* Eben?" Corey, who was nearly as jumpy as he was himself, tugged at Eben's sleeve and nodded at the clock. The minute hand had finally moved. It was closing time.

He locked the door after the last customer and turned to find Lilah rubbing the back of her neck. She smiled stiffly at him.

"That was a busy afternoon! So many customers, and they've left things in such a mess. Bethany and I have our work cut out for us, putting it all right before we leave for the day." She smiled down at the little girl, who smiled happily back. Bethany didn't know about the surprise, since Corey had warned Eben that his sister wasn't good at keeping secrets.

"Before you get started on that, let's all go out back," Eben suggested.

"Out back?" Lilah was rummaging under the counter for the dusting supplies she kept there. She tickled Bethany's nose with the feather duster. "Why?"

Corey made an impatient noise. "You can't ask questions. It's s'posed to be a surprise."

Bethany squealed and bounced up and down on her dirty tennis shoes. "A surprise, *Aent* Lilah! Let's go see what it is!"

Lilah looked uncertain, but she nodded. "All right."

Eben felt as nervous as a bridegroom as he led the way through the storeroom and opened the back door.

"There," he said awkwardly. "That's for you."

Lilah cast a puzzled look up at his face as she walked out into the sunshine. And then she stopped short and stared.

A well-polished wooden bench sat against the brick wall of the store. Maybe that wasn't so special itself, although he'd made certain it was sturdy made and would hold up well to the weather.

But he'd tried to make it special—best he could. He held his breath, waiting for her to notice.

Corey wasn't so patient.

"See?" The boy walked up to the bench and pointed. "There's butterflies carved all over. *Onkel* Eben had the man do it special 'cause you like butterflies so much."

Lilah looked up at him. "Because I like butterflies," she repeated slowly.

"You said you did," he reminded her. "The first day you worked here. You said you liked to sit and watch them."

He'd never paid much attention to butterflies before, but since Lilah had come along, he seemed to see them everywhere. And they always made him smile because they reminded him of her.

But right now, she was staring at the bench as if she'd never said a word about butterflies in her whole life.

"It's so pretty!" Bethany ran to the bench and hopped up on it. "Come sit with me, *Aent* Lilah, and try it out."

Lilah walked to the bench, but instead of sitting, she traced one of the fluttering carvings with one finger. "Because I like butterflies."

She sounded all right, but there was a suspicious looking sparkle in her eyes. Tears. Happy ones? Or sad? He couldn't tell.

"Corey, you and Bethany go on back inside," he said. "I want to talk to Lilah for a second."

"Okay!" Bethany said cheerfully, jumping down from the bench. "Do you like your surprise, *Aent* Lilah?"

Lilah gave the child a wobbly smile. "It's a real pretty bench, ain't so? *Denki*, Eben. And Corey," she added politely.

Eben waited until the children were inside the store before he spoke.

"It's for you to sit on when you come outside for lunch," he pointed out. "That other one was old and a little splintery. I thought this would be nicer."

"It's very nice. It's just that..."

"What's wrong?" He braced herself.

"Nothing. Only—" She took in a breath and turned to face him. "I don't know that I'll have much opportunity to sit here."

He didn't like the sound of that. "Why not?"

"Because I'm giving notice. I...can't work here much longer."

He stared at her. "*Vass?* Why?"

She'd dropped her eyes to her hands, folded in front of her dress. "I need to focus on my quilting. I've...figured out that I really do like quilting best, and I'm getting so many orders now. If I work hard enough, I'll be able to pay my living expenses that way. I hope you'll keep allowing me to sell my quilts in your store. Not," she added quickly, "for nothing, since I won't be working here anymore. But we could work out a percentage, maybe. If you'd be willing. If you're not willing, I understand."

Eben was tempted to say no. He wanted to say no because maybe if he did, she'd keep working here, where he could see her every day.

But that would be wrong. So he took a minute to steady himself before he answered. "*Ja*, we can do that. If you're sure you don't want to work here anymore." He paused. "Is that really what you want, Lilah?"

She didn't answer right away, and a tiny hope stirred in his heart.

"Because," he went on, "you don't have to quit if you don't want to. We could cut down your hours, if you wanted, so's you'd have more time for the quilting."

She shook her head. "*Nee*, you need somebody here full-time to help. You'll work yourself to death otherwise." She drew in a broken breath. "But it won't be hard to find some-body to take my place. Anna Speicher would be a good choice, I think."

"Anna?"

"She needs an income, and she'd be good at this sort of thing. She's a quick learner, and she gets along with peo-ple. And she could leave Matthew with Mary during work hours, I'm sure."

Why was she prattling on about poor Anna Speicher?

"I'm sure Anna would do all right, but I'd rather not—" He wasn't sure how to finish that sentence. *Rather not spend my days with anybody other than you.* "Rather not have to train a new worker right now."

"Oh, I can train her if you get her in soon enough. It won't take long." Lilah lifted her chin. "Now I'd best get inside." She flashed a quick smile that didn't quite reach her eyes. "Bethany's learning how to dust real well, but she still knocks things over sometimes."

She pulled the back door open, then paused. "And don't worry about the bench. It was a kind thought, and you didn't waste your money. You were right about that other one. It was about to fall apart."

Then she hurried inside, leaving him alone.

He had things to do himself. He was behind on his work

because he'd wasted time today picking up Lilah's gift. The sensible thing to do would be to go back into the store and get busy.

Instead he sat down on the bench with a sigh.

That hadn't gone so well. Either he was even more out of practice courting women than he'd thought, or for once in her life, Lilah had said something she didn't mean.

Maybe she didn't wish they could all be a family, after all.

Chapter Fourteen

$\sim$

Later that afternoon, Lilah stood in her bedroom studying the quilt she'd just spread over her bed. Rose's story quilt was perfectly clean now and beautiful.

It was also completed—down to the last stitch.

She hadn't intended to finish it. Not at first. She'd only planned to wash it. But when she'd brought it home, Susie had taken one look and tsked her tongue.

"I don't know, Lilah. It's going to need a real *gut* scrubbing. And unfinished like that—won't it be ruined?"

"I'm afraid it might," she'd confessed. "I promised to wash it, but I'm worried about it bunching up. If it were finished, there'd be no problem, but—"

"Then finish it," Susie had suggested. "You're as skilled with your needle as Rose was. You could do the job well, and then it would be a nice piece for him to save instead of just a sad memory."

"I've no idea, though, how she planned to finish it."

"*Nee*, we can't know that. Whatever plans Rose had, it was not *Gott*'s will that she complete them." Susie leaned closer. "There are roses on the fabric. Why not quilt a flower pattern over it? That'd be a nice reminder of her little garden, the one you like so much out behind the store. You could add some butterflies in there as well. I think that would be real pretty."

So Lilah had done exactly that. And it had turned out just as pretty as Susie had thought it would.

But now she had to return it to Eben, and with everything so jumbled up between them, she had no idea what he'd say or think.

"Stop fretting," Susie ordered from the doorway. "If Eben's mad, tell him to come fuss at me. Finishing the quilt was my idea."

She sure didn't seem particularly bothered. In fact, Susie had been surprisingly cheerful today. When Lilah had arrived home this afternoon and told her about giving notice at the store, she'd expected that Susie would want an explanation.

She'd been relieved when her friend had only shrugged and sighed.

Because how could she explain this? She couldn't even understand it herself.

But there was no doubt about it. The minute she'd seen that bench waiting in the little garden, seen the soft, hopeful light in his eyes as he waited for her reaction, she'd known.

She loved Eben Miller with all her heart. Maybe he cared for her, too—or thought he did. But she wasn't the right woman for him. She could never make him happy.

And he deserved to be happy.

Susie walked in and stood beside Lilah, looking down at the quilt. "I don't think you have anything to worry about. If Eben has any sense, he'll be pleased. You've done a good job. I can't tell which stitches are yours and which are Rose's. Why don't you put it in a pillowcase for safe carrying? I have some old ones in the linen closet that should do."

"*Denki*. And Susie? It won't fit in my scooter basket

very well, so could you give me a ride into town to deliver it? Maybe not this Friday but next?"

That would be her last day. Maybe the timing was a bit cowardly, but that day would be so hard anyhow. If Eben was upset with her, it might make leaving easier.

"I'll be happy to drive you, if it comes to that," Susie murmured vaguely. "Now, I'd better get back downstairs. I have a cake baking. You've had a troubling day. A little something sweet and a cup of tea after supper will be just the thing to cheer you up."

Susie pattered down the stairs. Lilah found the spare pillowcase and began folding the quilt.

It would fit, easily. The batting Rose had chosen was thin. This quilt wasn't made for snuggling under during cold nights, but rather for memories.

"You needn't have worried," she murmured as she tucked it inside the pillowcase. "He'll always remember you, even if he marries again. And you'd want him to do that—to marry and have a family and be happy again. Because when you love someone, you want them to be happy."

"Lilah? Can you come downstairs, please?"

Susie's call startled her out of her thoughts. She was embarrassed to realize she had tears on her cheeks, and she wiped them away as she set down the packaged quilt.

"Coming, Susie!" Lilah hurried down the stairs—and stopped short.

Eben stood in the kitchen. His face was pale, but determination glittered in his blue-gray eyes.

"Eben stopped by." Susie stood by the sink, a mixing bowl in her hand. Apparently she'd been caught in the middle of washing up, but she didn't look annoyed.

She looked amused.

"Why?" That was the only word Lilah could manage.

Eben shot a glance toward Susie, who'd turned her back, pretending to focus on wiping the bowl dry. "Maybe we should talk outside."

Lilah hesitated, but there didn't seem to be any way out of it. "All right," she agreed. She followed him out of the door and down the steps into the backyard.

But that was as far as she went. As soon as her shoes hit the grass, she stopped.

"Why are you here, Eben?" She held her breath waiting for his answer. Was he going to ask her not to stop working at the store? Or was there…something else he wanted to talk about?

Whatever it was, it was important enough to bring him all the way out here.

He turned to face her. "I brought the bench."

She blinked "What?"

"I had it made for you, so it's yours. I'd have been here sooner, but I had to take it apart to get it in the buggy." He sounded irritated.

That was all this was about? A bench? Lilah lifted her chin.

"You should have kept it at the store. Like I said, the other one's falling apart."

"It's yours," he repeated stubbornly. "Just tell me where to put it."

Lilah had learned a lot about Eben after all these weeks of working together. He was the kindest fellow in the county, but once he set his jaw like that, he wasn't budging. She could stand in the yard and argue with him all she liked, but that bench wasn't going back to the store.

She sighed and considered. "Maybe under the plum tree. It would look real pretty there, and there'll be some shade."

"It'd be pretty, maybe, but not so practical for sitting.

You'll have fruit falling on your head in the summertime, and wasps buzzing around, too, most likely. If you want it under a tree, that old oak over there would be a smarter pick."

"Fine. Put it there."

Eben went to the buggy and began unloading parts of the bench. It seemed to be in a good many pieces.

"How long is it going to take you to put it together?"

"Not long."

"Well, I'd say I hate to put you to the trouble except that I'm not the one troubling you."

Eben set the seat of the bench on the ground under the oak and looked at her. "The bench was meant to be my gift to you, Lilah. I'm sorry you don't like it."

"Of course I like it!"

Eben started back to the buggy for another piece of bench. "Then it's me you don't like, I reckon."

"Don't be silly." She tried her best to sound casual—as if they were talking about something no more important than the weather. "I like you fine."

"It sure doesn't seem so."

He was on his way back to the tree again now, carrying the back of the bench with its butterfly decorations. Her heart thudded hard.

"Well, you're mistaken, then," she muttered. "I'm not leaving the store because I don't like you, Eben." It was exactly the opposite, but that wasn't something he needed to know. "I need to spend more time on my quilting."

He shot her a sharp look. "Is that the truth?"

It was the truth. Or part of it. Lilah tried to think of how best to answer.

"Because if it is, I have an idea." He'd gone back to collect the metal side pieces of the bench, and he dropped them on the soft ground with a thud. "You could do your quilting at the store."

"What?"

"We could set you up over in the old quilting corner, and you could sew during our slow times. Rose used to do that sometimes. That's why the frame was set up there. Customers would likely love to see you at work. Of course, we could run a little rope across the doorway when you are busy, maybe, to keep them from pestering you."

Lilah shook her head. "I don't think that would be a good idea."

"Why not?" He dumped another armload of parts on the grass. "Why are you quitting me, Lilah?"

"I told you. I can't work at the store and get all my quilting done."

"I didn't ask you why you were quitting the store." Leaving the bits of bench on the ground, he walked over until he was standing right in front of her. "I asked you why you were quitting *me*."

"I don't—I don't know what you mean." She felt flustered.

"I think maybe you do," he said gently. "I had plenty of time to think while I was taking this bench apart. There's a reason why it was so sturdy. It was a job to take it apart, let me tell you. And the whole time I was working on it, I was thinking about you."

"You...you were?"

"I was thinking about what a smart woman you are. And wondering how come you hadn't figured out why I went to the trouble to buy this bench for you. Why I had it special made with butterflies because you like them. I was feeling pretty *dumm*, let me tell you. But I'm not *dumm*. And neither are you. You've got to know, Lilah. You've got to

know I've come to care about you as more than a friend."
He waited, holding her eyes with his. "Don't you?"

"I…" she trailed off helplessly. She couldn't lie, so she
didn't say anything else.

"Ja." He nodded, and that muscle jumped in his jaw.
"You know."

"Eben—" she started, but she couldn't figure out what
to say next.

"So," he went on, "either you don't feel the same way
about me, and you're trying to let me down easy-like—and
not doing a real *gut* job of it, by the way. Or you do care,
and you've got some silly reason in your head about why
we shouldn't be together." He crossed his arms in front of
his chest. "So that's what I've come to find out, and I'm
not leaving until I do. Which is it?"

As he asked the question, he straightened his shoulders—just a little. Someone else might not even have noticed it, but she noticed everything about Eben. She knew
what that little gesture meant. He was bracing himself—as
if he needed to protect his heart from her answer.

*Please, Gott, for once in my life. Let me say the right
thing.*

She took a deep breath and looked him in the eye. "It's
not a silly reason."

Eben's eyes widened, and then to her surprise, he
laughed—the laugh of a man on the first day of spring
after a long, hard winter.

"You *do* care for me," he said, stepping closer. He crooked
a finger under her chin, tilting it up. He looked deep into her
eyes as if trying to decide if he could believe what he was
hearing. Whatever he saw must have satisfied him because
he smiled, an amazed, incredulous smile.

"You care," he repeated.

And then he kissed her.

* * *

If a man could spend a summer afternoon kissing Lilah Troyer, Eben didn't think he'd ever want to do anything else. But there were still some things to settle between them, still some important words to say, so finally—reluctantly—he lifted his lips from hers.

Her eyes fluttered open, and she looked up at him, her face prettily flushed. He waited, but she said nothing.

He smiled. "Seems like I've finally found a way to get you to stop talking."

She blinked, and the dazed joy faded from her face. She took a step backward—an unsteady one. He caught her elbow as she wobbled.

"Careful," he said.

"You shouldn't…you shouldn't have done that."

"You don't think so?" He lifted an eyebrow. "And here I am thinking I should have done it a lot sooner."

"This isn't funny, Eben." She still looked flustered, but he could see that she was trying to gather her wits. "You can't… I don't…"

She faltered to a stop.

"I think we've just found out that I can, and that you do, Lilah. If I had any doubts at all that you cared for me, they're gone now. You'd never have let me kiss you, otherwise. So tell me this silly reason of yours, and let's get it out of the way. Why do you think you can't marry me?"

"*Marry* you?"

He laughed at the shock in her voice. "Would I go around kissing women I'm not planning to marry? At my age? The bishop would likely have something to say about that, don't you think?"

He was teasing her, and the trick worked. A spark flashed into her eyes. "Well, forgive me for being a little surprised, but it's a good-sized jump from a first kiss to a marriage proposal."

"At our age, we've no time to waste. I want you to marry me, Lilah. As soon as we can manage it. That much is settled. The question is, do you want to marry me?"

She'd been looking up into his face this whole time, as if she couldn't believe what she was hearing. But now she looked away, staring over the rolling pastures behind Susie's home as the last of the just-kissed color faded out of her face.

"Lilah." He tried to gently tilt her face back toward his, but she jerked free. "What is it? Don't you want to marry me?"

She didn't answer, and he could have kicked himself. He'd bumbled this whole thing. He'd not been thinking clearly—Lilah had that effect on him.

But that was no excuse.

He had to remember, Lilah had never been married. This was all new to her, so of course it would come as a shock. He doubted she'd ever even been kissed before, and here he was, dropping everything on her at once.

He should have gone more slowly. Said prettier words, given her time. Not driven up in her yard with a bench all taken to pieces and kissed her right out of the blue.

"I'm sorry, sweetheart," he murmured. "I don't mean to rush you. Let's start over. You said your reason wasn't silly."

"It isn't."

"Tell me what it is then, and let's talk about it."

He couldn't imagine any *gut* reason why he and Lilah shouldn't be together. But clearly she thought she had one, so he'd hear her out.

And then he planned on kissing her again.

"So?" he prodded gently. "What is it?"

"I'm not the right woman for you," Lilah blurted out.

Ja, that was a real silly reason, all right. If she hadn't seemed so miserable, he'd have laughed out loud.

"I think I'm the one who gets to decide that. And anyhow, you're mistaken. I promise you, you're exactly the right woman for me."

"I'm not." She shook her head stubbornly. "I'm too old."

He frowned. "What on earth are you talking about? You're younger than I am."

"Not young enough," Lilah was saying. "You'd be better off with someone else. Someone like Anna Speicher. She already has a son. You'd have a family, Eben. Right away, and—"

"Lilah? I don't want to hear another word about me marrying Anna Speicher."

"But—"

"Not another word," he said firmly. "You're the woman I'm in love with, and you're the only woman I've any interest in marrying. If you don't love me back, you should be honest enough to say so."

"Of course I love you back." Lilah fisted her hands on her hips.

His heart leaped into his throat. "Then—" he said, stepping closer.

But she took another step back. "And that's why I can't marry you."

He was starting to feel desperate. "Because you love me? You're not making sense."

"Love means always wanting the best for the other person. I'm not the best for you."

He'd had enough of this. He took a slow, deliberate step forward, closing the gap between them. "Lilah, I'm not an arguing sort of a man."

"That doesn't mean you're not stubborn." She took another step backward.

"But," he went on as if she hadn't spoken. "This is worth arguing about. You are the best for me, Lilah. You're sweet. You're smart." He took a step forward. She backed up. "You're strong." Two more steps, first his, then hers. "You make me laugh. Before you came along, do you know how long it had been since I'd laughed? A very…" He took a tiny step. She didn't move. "Very long time." Another tiny step. "And you're beautiful, too."

"Beautiful." She made a scoffing sound. "I thought we were being honest."

"I *am* being honest." He reached up to trace the curve of her cheek. "You are beautiful, Lilah. And not just on the outside, but on the inside, where it really matters. You're always finding some way to help people. Like washing Rose's quilt for me."

"Oh." She blinked. "About the quilt—"

He didn't want to talk about that quilt. Not right now. So he went on as if she hadn't spoken. "And making all those lunches for me and Corey and Bethany."

Her face changed. "The children."

"*Ja*, them. And—"

"That's the problem." Tears glittered in her lashes. He'd been planning to take another step forward, but those tears stopped him in his tracks. Lilah wasn't the kind of woman who cried easily. "You love children, Eben Miller. You know you do."

She made it sound like an accusation. "Of course I do."

"And you'd be happiest with a houseful of them, like the Fishers have. You deserve a family like that, Eben. You'd be such a good *vadder*. But I'm…" She swallowed. "I'm going to be forty on my next birthday."

Ah. So that was what this was about.

"Forty's not old, Lilah," he said gently.

"*Mamm* became a grandmother when she was forty-two."

"So she got an earlier start. Ruth Fisher's the same age as you are," he pointed out. "And she and Mark aren't packing their cradle away quite yet, I notice."

"But what if—"

"What if?" He captured her hands in his. "There's no point asking that question. Trust me, I know. I've asked it a thousand times. There's never any answer. We can't know, Lilah. *Gott* gives us plenty to manage, but there are some things we have to leave in His hands. We have to trust Him. Don't we?"

She nodded mutely.

"Of course we do. We have to believe that if He wants us to have a family, He'll bless us with one."

"And if..." She swallowed. "And if He doesn't?"

He brought her hands to his lips and kissed them. "Then we'll have each other. And if that's truly the Lord's will for us, it will be more than enough."

"Oh," she whispered. "Do you really think so, Eben?"

"I know this," he said. "If a certain sweet, smart, beautiful woman will stop arguing with me for once in her life and just say yes, I'll be the happiest man alive."

He waited while Lilah stared up into his face for one long moment.

One long, excruciatingly silent moment.

"Lilah?" he prompted. "It's your turn to talk now."

"Don't rush me." Her brow puckered. "I don't... I don't know what to say. I mean. I know what I *want* to say. I just don't know *how* to say it right."

His lips twitched. Even when she was stretching his heart—and his patience—to its limits, this woman could still make him smile.

"Then I'll tell you what to say. Say 'Yes, Eben. Yes, I love you, and I will marry you, and we'll eat lunch and watch butterflies together for the rest of our days.'"

She tilted her face, and now a teasing twinkle sparkled alongside the tears in her eyes. "I do love you, Eben Miller, but if you think you'll get to tell me what to say just because we're getting married, you'd best think again. And if you don't carry this bench right back to the store where it belongs, we'll be eating all those butterfly lunches sitting on the ground."

He grinned. "Close enough."

And then he kissed her again.

Epilogue

A little over a year later, Lilah stood on tiptoes in the spare bedroom of her and Eben's home, rummaging through the linens she'd stored on the top shelf of the closet.

She was sure she'd put Rose's quilt up here when they'd moved in last fall, just after their marriage. Well, almost sure. She'd been pleasantly distracted by her handsome new husband and the joy of finally having a home of her own to fuss over.

A home of her very own. Eben had insisted on selling the house he and Rose had shared and buying a different one—one he and Lilah had chosen together.

She'd told him, more than once, that she'd not have minded living in the old house, but Eben wouldn't hear of it. "This is a new beginning for both of us," he'd said. "I think we should start fresh."

In the end, they had bought a nice little farmhouse just down the road from Susie's. It wasn't far from the store, either. Their new life had started off very well.

Hopefully it was about to get even better. But first, there was something she needed to take care of.

She finally spied the package she was looking for, underneath a pile of extra sheets. She pulled down the pillowcase containing the folded quilt just as the kitchen door downstairs banged.

She smiled. Eben was in from the barn already. He'd gotten the morning chores done in record time.

And no wonder. Today was going to be a very special day.

"Lilah?" Her husband's deep voice drifted up. "Where are you?"

"Upstairs! But I'm coming down," she called back. "There's something I have to show you."

She bundled the quilt up in her arms and started down the steps. Eben was in the kitchen, prizing open the tin of cookies she'd put on the table.

"Eben Miller!" she scolded. "Those cookies are for the *kinder* and the social worker."

"There's plenty to spare." He winked at her and smiled. "You and Susie have made enough treats to welcome twenty foster children, and we're only expecting two. Surely a hungry husband can steal a few."

"You can eat all the cookies you want," she told him, pretending that wink and that mischievous smile didn't turn her insides to mush—which they always did. "So long as you wash your hands before you go scrabbling about in the tin. If our social worker finds a wisp of hay—or worse— on her cookie when she brings Corey and Bethany by this afternoon, she's likely to tell us we can't be their foster parents after all."

"Corey and Bethany's parents." Eben's smile widened as he went over to the sink to scrub his hands. "I like the sound of that."

"*Foster* parents," she reminded him. "At least for now. And I'm glad to hear it suits you, considering after today we'll have two *kinder* running about this house. And maybe some more, after that."

She waited, holding her breath, but Eben simply continued drying his hands on the blue-and-white-striped towel.

"I want to foster more children, *ja*," he said. "Although, maybe not right away. I know there are plenty more little ones who need homes, and I like the idea of us having a passel of them here. But I think Corey and Bethany may need a while being the only ones. They've gone without so much for so long. It may take some time to fill their hearts up."

"They can be the only ones for a while, I suppose," Lilah agreed, watching her husband closely. "Maybe six months or so."

"*Ja*, that would be about right. By then, the adoption should be moving well along, and Corey and Bethany will feel more settled."

Lilah smothered a sigh. Eben was proving immune to her hints, but maybe that was for the best. Today was going to be exciting enough. She could keep her secret a little longer.

Maybe.

"Hopefully that'll be the case, now that Corey and Bethany's parents have signed those papers giving up their rights," she said. "But remember, the social worker warned us that adoptions always seem to take longer than you'd expect. Lots of red tape, she said."

Eben returned to the table and reached for the cookie tin. "I won't mind waiting, so long as Corey and Bethany are ours at the end of things." He poked through the selection of fresh cookies, and Lilah noticed that he chose two of the ones she'd made herself.

"Susie's cookies taste better," she reminded him. It was true. She was a decent baker, but Susie had an expert touch with such things.

"I like yours best." Another wink. "What's that?" As he took a bite of cookie, Eben nodded at the bundled quilt she'd laid on the table.

She'd nearly forgotten. "It's what I wanted to show you. Eat your cookies first, though."

"Uh-oh. Trying to butter me up?"

She made a face at him, but there was some truth to it. She wasn't entirely sure how Eben was going to react. In fact, she suddenly wondered if it had been such a good idea to pull the quilt down this morning, after all. She didn't want him to be upset, not today of all days.

But it had seemed important—to her at least—to do this now. She wanted to get this smudge off her conscience.

"You stay pretty well buttered, I think. I just don't want you to get crumbs all over it."

"Over what?"

"Finish up, then come on out to the living room, and I'll show you." She bundled the quilt into her arms and carried it out of the kitchen.

Once in their living room, she pulled it out of the pillow-case and spread it over the sofa, checking it carefully. The inspection didn't take long. Rose's quilt was just as clean and perfect as it had been when she'd folded it away last summer.

The day Eben had asked her to marry him. A smile tickled her lips at the memory.

So much had happened since then. So many happy and wonderful things. And, of course, some not so happy ones, too.

As she'd feared, Bethany and Corey's placement with the Johnsons hadn't lasted—and she and Eben had been partly the cause of that. After thinking it over and spending some time in prayer, they'd decided to contact the local social services agency and share their concerns about the lack of care the children were receiving.

They'd been asked to come into the office, and they'd been *naerfich*. Neither of them knew much about the foster care system. But the social worker they'd met with had been pleasant and kind, and she'd seemed genuinely upset about Corey and Bethany's situation.

"I've had some concerns about the placement, myself," she'd admitted. "I'd have moved them already if I could have. But there's such a shortage of foster parents in this area, particularly those willing to take on sibling groups. It'll mean moving them out of the county, so they'll have to change schools." She sighed. "We hate to do that, but sometimes there's just no choice."

Lilah had opened her mouth to say that it was a shame, but Eben spoke before she could. "What does a person have to do? To be a foster parent? Could a Plain couple like us do it?"

"Yes," the woman had answered immediately, her eyes lighting up. "Absolutely. Of course, there's a lot you'll have to do first, classes and home inspections and such. It's a good bit of work."

Eben had only laughed. "That's one thing about us Amish. We're never afraid of hard work. How do we get started?"

Lilah had barely heard the social worker's answer. She'd been too busy staring at her new husband—her wonderful husband who had enough room in his heart for a dozen foster children, at least.

So, armed with a folder full of information, and after a great deal more prayer and a consultation with the bishop, they'd started on the process to become foster parents. The social worker had told them the truth. It was a lot of work. But today—finally—they'd be welcoming Corey and Bethany home.

"Rose's story quilt." Eben stood in the kitchen doorway. As he walked over to look at it, Lilah held her breath, trying to read the expression on his face. "I haven't thought about that for months. Why do you have it out?"

"Because." She swallowed, hard. "I have a confession to make. I finished it."

"You did what?"

"Right after you gave it to me to wash. I finished up the quilting. I should have told you sooner, but—there was so much going on." She sucked in a guilty breath. "And honestly, I was afraid to. I thought maybe you'd be mad. That you might change your mind and not want to marry me after all."

Her husband snorted. "Not likely." He leaned down to get a closer look. "What is this pattern here on the edge of it? The part you sewed—that's flowers, isn't it?"

"*Ja*, it is." Lilah bit her lip. "It's…roses and butterflies."

"Roses and butterflies." He glanced up at her, and she hurried to explain.

"It was Susie's idea. She thought it would be a sweet reminder of Rose's garden out back of the store, and I liked the idea. It wasn't until later that… I didn't realize, Eben. Truly, I didn't. Not until you gave me that bench, and by then the quilting was already done."

Eben had straightened and was watching her. "Realize what?"

She flushed. "That butterflies made you think of me. If I'd known, I'd not have sewn them on there. I honestly didn't mean to put anything of myself on Rose's quilt, and I'm sure Susie didn't mean to, either."

To her surprise, Eben's mouth quirked. "I wouldn't be so certain of that. She's quite the matchmaker, our Susie."

"You're not angry?"

"*Nee*, sweetheart, I am not angry." He spoke quietly, his gaze still on the quilt.

"I probably should have left it alone. It was just so dusty, Eben, and there was no way to clean it safely unless the border was finished. The batting would have bunched— and—"

"Stop explaining." He put his arm around her, drawing her close against his side. He smelled like her good laundry soap—and the barn—and a little like cookies. "I'm glad you did it." He sighed. "When Rose started this quilt, her health was already bad. She'd no energy for such a job, but she wanted to make it as a gift for me. She prayed and prayed that she'd be allowed to finish it." He cleared his throat. "I'm ashamed to admit that I questioned *Gott* about many things during that time, and that was one of them. Why couldn't He have let Rose finish her quilt? It seemed such a small thing, and it meant so much to her. But now I think I see why He didn't."

"What?" Lilah looked up into her husband's kind face. "What is it that you see?"

"That maybe finishing this quilt was your job to do." He leaned down and traced the stitching with a finger. "No one else could have done it so well. We all leave things undone at the end, ain't so? Someone else will pick up our needle or our shovel or our pen, and they will finish what we started. And maybe that is not such a sad thing. Because they will bring their own strength to the jobs we leave behind, add their own beauty, like you've done here."

"And like we'll do, you and me," Lilah whispered. "With Corey and Bethany. They were born to another family, but we will finish the job of bringing them up."

She felt her husband's muscles flex as he drew her even closer against him. "*Ja*, that we will, as best we can. And we'll do the same for other children, too, if *Gott* wills it. Although—" he rested his chin on the top of her *kapp*

"—maybe we should hold off on that until after the *boppli* comes."

"Eben!" Lilah drew back to look into his face. Blue-gray eyes twinkled at her. "You know?"

"I've known since you slipped off for that first doctor's appointment. I've been wondering when you'd get around to telling me." He lifted an eyebrow. "I've tried to be patient, but it's taken a lot longer than I expected. Usually, you're not so *gut* at keeping quiet."

She swatted him. "I wanted to wait until it seemed likely things would go well. I just… I didn't want to disappoint you."

"*Vass?* You could never disappoint me, Lilah Miller." He pulled her close again. "Surprise me? Argue with me until I want to bite a nail in half? Make me happier than any man deserves to be? *Ja*, those things you do, every single day. But disappoint me? Never."

"You make me happy, too, Eben Miller." Lilah closed her eyes and leaned her head against her husband's chest, comforted by the steady, reassuring thump of his heart.

Then she frowned.

"But I don't argue with you," she said, her voice muffled by his shirt. "At least, not every day. You're wrong about that."

"Really?" Under her cheek, her husband's teasing laughter rumbled. "Am I?"

Pulling away, she fisted her hands on her hips. "Eben!"

That was as far as she got before he tipped up her chin and kissed her frown away.

* * * * *

Dear Reader,

Do you feel like life is moving too fast these days? Wish you could slow down a little bit? No worries—I've got the perfect remedy! Pour yourself a nice cup of tea, find your favorite reading chair and slip away with me to the Amish community of Hickory Springs, Tennessee.

Hickory Springs is the perfect place to relax and de-stress. In this peaceful small town, family is treasured, faith forms the foundation of every decision—and love is in full bloom.

You'll meet fascinating folks here, people who will quickly feel like friends. There's outspoken quilter Lilah Troyer, brokenhearted storekeeper Eben Miller—and, of course, their unofficial matchmaker Susie Raber, who specializes in unexpected happily-ever-afters!

The Amish Widower's Surprise is my very first Amish story for Love Inspired, and I'm already looking forward to more visits to Hickory Springs. I hope you are, too!

In the meantime, let's stay in touch! Head over to laurelblountbooks.com and sign up to be a part of my favorite bunch of folks—my beloved newsletter subscribers! Every month, I share photos, book news and gotta-try-it recipes. And, of course, you can always write to me at laurelblountwrites@gmail.com!

I look forward to hearing from you!

Much love,
Laurel